UNBUTTONED & EXPOSED

A Collection of Gay Erotica Short Stories

by Gray Wilder

FRANKLIN
PUBLISHERS

Disclaimer

Table of Contents

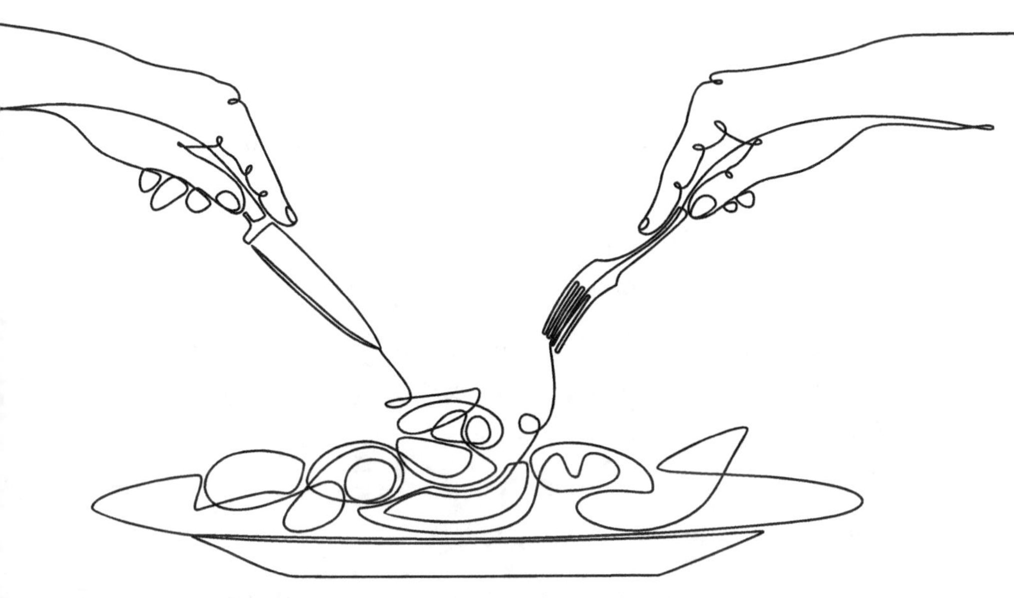

1: Dinner With a Friend

"Can I add mushrooms?" John asked, his voice as casual as if he were suggesting a salad dressing. He stood at the counter, holding a carton of them up like a rare artifact.

Alec blinked, caught off guard by the question. "Sure... but why ask?"

"Some people hate mushrooms," John replied with a shrug. "And I'm not about forcing fungus on anyone."

Alec's lips twitched into a rare smile, the kind John always tried to coax out of him. "Fungus doesn't bother me. I'm pro-mushroom."

John grinned. "Good man. Mostly, I am too. Mostly." He furrowed his brow. "Except for Bella mushrooms. They taste like mold. No matter what I do."

Alec tilted his head, raised a finger like he was about to make a grand revelation, then promptly shut his mouth.

John rolled his eyes dramatically. "Yes, yes, I know. Technically, mushrooms are mold," he said, mocking a lecture with a playful smirk. "But, seriously, Bella mushrooms taste like... well, like the underside of a wet log."

Alec chuckled, his amusement quickly giving way to curiosity. "What are these mushrooms going into, exactly?"

John, now rummaging through the fridge, emerged triumphantly with a medley of vegetables, soy sauce, and a bottle of lime juice. "I call it... John's Noodles." He flourished a pack of pasta like it was a sacred scroll.

Alec's brow furrowed. "Is it good?"

John paused, pondering this. "No idea. Every time, it's a bit different. I just go with whatever 'feels right'." He made air quotes around the last words, a glint of mischief in his eyes as he started filling a pot with water.

Alec muttered under his breath, "Fascinating."

John paused mid-pour, raising an eyebrow. "That's a weird word for someone's cooking." He tapped his chin with mock thoughtfulness. "Was hoping for something more along the lines of 'mouthwatering' or 'culinary genius.' But hey, I'll take it."

Alec shook his head, a soft smile tugging at his lips. "It's just... I usually have a recipe card, so I know what the final dish should be. I like to know where I'm going."

"Too organized," John declared, already slicing mushrooms and tomatoes with a casual lack of precision. He tossed them into the browning ground turkey, adding a splash of wine directly from his own glass, lime juice, and soy sauce without so much as glancing at a measuring cup.

Alec stared wide-eyed, taking a sip from his wine glass as he glared over the rim. "You're not... you're not measuring any of that?"

John grinned, throwing a wink Alec's way. "Nah. Cooking's an art, not a science. Besides, it'll be delicious. Trust me."

Alec crossed his arms skeptically. "Has it always been delicious?"

John let out a dramatic sigh, shaking his head as if explaining a universal truth. "Of course not. Good judgment comes from experience... and experience? Well, experience comes from bad judgment." He shot Alec a quick glance, waiting for the reaction.

The laugh that escaped Alec surprised even him. John, victorious, smiled, his chest warming at the sound. He always loved getting Alec to laugh. It didn't happen often enough, and when it did, it was like a small victory, proof that the world wasn't always so serious. They had only known each other for a few months, but their friendship had developed quickly and intensely.

As the noodles boiled and John worked his magic, Alec watched him closely—his messy energy a strange yet compelling contrast to his own neat, calculated world. Alec poured more wine into his glass and waited patiently for the final product.

A few minutes later, John dished up two plates, carefully folded a dish towel neatly over his forearm, and handed one to Alec with a flourish as if presenting a five-star meal at a fancy restaurant.

Alec hesitated, fork hovering over the haphazard creation, but after the first bite, his eyes widened. "This is amazing," he declared a note of wonder in his voice. "I wasn't sure about the lime juice, wine, and soy sauce with tomatoes, but... it works. It's weird, but it works."

John grinned to himself, slurping a noodle with a satisfied hum. He liked having Alec around more than he'd expected. This was the first time he'd cooked for him, and it felt like something clicked. Maybe he didn't need a recipe card after all—not for this, anyway.

After they cleaned their plates, Alec helped John wash the dishes, standing side by side at the sink without talking. Occasionally, they would look out the window at the brilliant sunset. Exchanged glances and mutual smiles, silently acknowledging their friendship.

"Let's chill on the couch and talk about our plans for the upcoming trip," John suggested. The conference was an unexpected bonus. They realized over lunch one day that they would both be attending the same event later that year. Alec knew that John was straight, and the attraction that he felt for him was pointless to explore. Nevertheless, fantasies played vividly in his mind.

"Good idea," Alec responded. "We should probably have a plan rather than treating it like your noodles."

John chuckled. "I don't approach everything like my cooking, Alec," John teased.

They refilled their wine glasses and settled on the long sofa. Alec stretched out his legs towards John, playfully punching John's leg with his toes before pulling his feet back under him. John laughed, turned his legs towards Alec, and kicked back.

"No kicking!" he said, laughing while continuing to kick towards Alec.

"So, what's the plan for this conference, chef John?" Alec asked.

They sat and talked about plans for where to go and what to see, which workshops and seminars to attend, which to skip, and where to eat. Conversation was casual and comfortable. Like two friends who had known each other for many years.

They talked about their plans, which included spending a few days in the city before traveling to the countryside to experience some local culture at a farm that sold ice cream made from the milk produced by a local dairy. As the conversation progressed, Alec stretched out on the couch, his feet extending once again towards John. John reached out casually, mid-sentence, and placed his hands on Alec's feet. Alec's heart skipped a beat with John's touch. Alec hated to have his feet touched.

Very few people had ever been able to touch his feet. Even during the occasional massage, he would warn the therapist to steer clear of the feet, or the session would be over. Alec felt John's touch oddly comforting, so he allowed it to continue.

After a few moments of his hand resting lightly on the bridge of Alec's left foot, John started to gently rub it, his hand occasionally venturing slightly up Alec's ankle. John continued to talk, seemingly unaware that his hand was sending a very strong message.

Alec inched towards John so that both feet rested in John's lap. John immediately placed both hands on Alec's feet and started to massage the soles, competently moving his fingers toward the toes and eventually between them. Alec released a low moan at the sensation.

"I'm sorry," John whispered. "Am I doing something wrong?"

"No, John, just the opposite," Alec whispered back. "What you're doing is perfect. I'm just not sure you know where this is headed."

John was quiet for a moment, and Alec was sure that this would be the end of the foot rub, as well as their friendship. John lifted Alec's right foot to his face and gently kissed his big toe. "I know exactly where this is headed, Alec," John replied quietly.

Alec sat up, his feet still in John's lap, placed his hand on the back of John's neck, and pulled him towards him. Alec's lips brushed gently against John's, pausing for a moment to make sure this was really happening. John pushed back firmly against Alec's open mouth, his tongue probing for Alec's.

John pushed Alec back and extended himself fully on top of Alec, their mouths never losing contact. John moved the kissing to Alec's cheek and down the side of his neck until his face and head were resting on the junction of Alec's chest and shoulder.

"I've wanted this for so long, Alec. I just didn't know how to let myself do it." John's words were full of emotion and relief.

"I've wanted this too, John. From the first moment I met you. Let's let this happen tonight and see where it goes. I don't want to think about it, I just want it." Alec's tone was firm. He had wanted this, and now he was going to have it. "Take your shirt off," he commanded.

John sat up, straddling Alec, and pulled his shirt off over his head. "His body is better than I imagined," Alec thought to himself. John's torso was athletic and muscular, a light dusting of hair across the top of his chest with more of the same on his belly. A thicker tuft of hair in the hollow of his throat gave the appearance that he was hairier than he really was. The pattern of hair, the perfect medium pink nipples, and John's solid musculature caused feelings in Alec that he had not felt in a very long time. Could this be what love felt like? Or was it just lust for something he previously thought unobtainable? Maybe all of the above, when combined with intense physical attraction?

Alec's hands rested on John's hips. He slowly moved them up to John's chest and lightly explored every inch, pausing slightly to spend some time on the nipples. This time, John moaned. "You found my sensitive spot," John said, looking Alec directly in the eyes. "Take your shirt off, Alec, then get back to what you were doing."

John helped Alec unbutton his short sleeve shirt and pull his arms out of the sleeves, leaving the shirt on the couch under them. John looked down at Alec. So many tattoos. So many lines.

Alec favored geometric tattoos. He had a large variety of ink. Most of his torso was covered in geometric patterns and various sayings in several languages. John took a finger and started tracing the patterns through the fur that covered Alec's chest, getting lost in the sensation of being able to touch something that he'd previously thought forbidden.

Satisfied with now having access to his body, John settled entirely on top of Alec, kissing him gently on the lips. Alec responded with increasing pressure, his lips pressing into John's with a fervor of a person who thought that what he held might be taken away at any moment.

John responded by forcing his tongue into Alec's open mouth. They kissed passionately, their hands exploring each other's bodies. Alec's hand slipped under John's shorts and firmly grabbed his firm ass cheeks, massaging them in rhythm with the kiss.

Abruptly, Alec pushed John up. "Stand up," Alec commanded.

"Did I do something wrong?" John responded.

"No, John. You're doing everything exactly right. I just want to enjoy this properly. Now stand up," Alec whispered, his voice firm yet kind.

John stood up, his attraction evident through the running shorts he was wearing.

Alec stood as well, the front of his track pants belying his body's reaction to touching John.

John and Alec stood, facing each other. Alec placed his hands on John's hips and pulled him close, holding him there tightly while he kissed him. John responded by placing his hands on Alec's upper back, feeling the light fur that covered even more complex tattoos. "I can't wait to explore his body," John thought to himself.

Alec halted the kiss and moved his hands to John's chest, moving his left hand to the shoulder while his right hand slowly moved down the center line of John's torso until it reached the waistband of his shorts. Alec paused briefly at the patch of hair on John's belly, his fingers gingerly touching the softness before hooking into the waistband of the shorts. Alec deftly slid two fingers of his right hand to the side of John's shorts as his left hand moved down his flank. With a smooth and definitive motion, Alec pulled the shorts down to John's ankles, squatting in coordination with the motion so that his face was level with John's crotch. Alec had often fantasized about this moment. The time when he would reveal what John's dick looked like. It was perfect. Alec had often been challenged on dates with other guys when this moment actually came. He did not care about size but rather was more sensitive to shape. John's was perfect for what Alec liked. On the smaller side, symmetrical with a well-defined and larger head. Alec's eagerness took over, and he launched himself into John's crotch, taking in John's intoxicating musk as his lips slid quickly down the shaft. John's size allowed Alec to take it all and still extend his tongue to gently caress John's balls. A loud moan escaped John's zips.

"Alec," John mumbled, "I've never felt anything like this."

Alec slowly withdrew his mouth and stood to face John. John leaned in for a kiss, tasting himself on Alec's lips. This turned him on more than he thought possible. John reached down and pulled the string to untie Alec's jogging pants. He fumbled as he tried to push them down, and Alec assisted to get them down to his ankles where he used his feet to remove them completely. John could feel Alec's rock-hard cock pulsing against his own. He reached down to touch it, something he had been wanting to do for a long time. Alec was well endowed. Much larger than John.

"You're so much bigger than me," John said quietly in Alec's ear.

"It's not about size," Alec replied. "You need to be okay with that. For me, yours is perfect."

John rested his head on the nape of Alec's neck and kissed there. "Thank you, Alec. You always know what to say."

"I'll always be honest with you. Always," Alec responded.

They held each other tightly for a moment, enjoying the sensations of their bodies pressed against one another. Alec then grabbed John firmly by the shoulders and moved him to the sofa, pushing him back into a seated position. Alec gently spread John's legs and knelt on the floor between them. He stroked John's chest as he moved his face back down to his waiting dick, his left hand settled on John's left nipple while his right assisted him taking care of John's arousal. It did not take long for John to reach climax. For John, the release was intense as he exploded in Alec's mouth. He moaned loudly as his body tensed briefly, then moved into extreme relaxation when it was over. Alec repositioned himself to sit on the sofa beside John. Alec extended his arm around John's shoulder and pulled his head to rest on his chest, softly stroking John's hair. They sat there for a few moments while John recovered.

"Now let me take care of you," John said. Alec leaned back as John's hand found Alec's ample dick. He stroked slowly, using his tongue to lick firmly at the nipple closest to his mouth. "Let me know if I can do anything differently."

"What you're doing is perfect," Alec replied.

John continued to stroke, his mouth moving from the nipple to Alec's mouth. John kissed so strongly, that it felt like electricity though Alec's entire body.

"I want to taste you," John said as he slid from the sofa to mimic Alec's positioning while he was taking care of him. John played with Alec, exploring, teasing, tasting. It was something he had never done. He learned quickly and approached it with a sense of enjoyment that surprised Alec. Alec continued to groan and moan as John hit all the right spots. How did he know what to do, and to do it so well? Alec did not care, he was immersed totally in the experience and allowed John to explore. Eventually, John moved back up the couch, never removing his hand from Alec's dick, which was now harder than ever. He stroked more quickly as he kissed Alec. From that moment, it didn't take long for Alec to finish. The explosion was unlike anything Alec had experienced in his significant amount of experience with other men. "This must be what it feels like to have this release coupled with deep emotion," he thought.

Spent, Alec collapsed on the couch. John settled to his side, running his hand through Alec's chest hair, his head resting quietly on Alec's shoulder.

"I need a snack!" John said suddenly.

"Fantastic idea," Alec agreed. "I could actually go for some of those leftover noodles."

"Seriously?" John questioned.

"Seriously," Alec responded. "They were delicious hot, and I think they would be even better cold. I love cold noodles!"

"Coming right up, buddy."

John got up, pulled on his shorts, and made his way to the kitchen. Returning a few minutes later with a single dish of noodles and two forks. They sat on the couch, side by side, slurping noodles, laughing, talking about how the mushrooms really made the dish.

"You're still naked," John said.

"I like being naked. Especially around you!" Alec retorted, laughing as he leaned over and planted a big, playful kiss on John's mouth, which had noodles partially extending from his lips.

After a few more bites, John took Alec's fork and made his way to the kitchen to place the dish and utensils in the sink. "Meet me in the bedroom," John commanded.

Alec needed no other encouragement. He jogged down the hall and threw himself on the bed. Naked and exposed, waiting for John.

John arrived soon after Alec. Round two was more intense than the first as both men put aside all inhibitions and allowed their mutual explorations of each other to proceed with the knowledge that they each wanted the same thing.

After they were both satisfied, Alec turned John to the right and spooned him, his tattooed arm embracing John's torso. Alec gently kissed him on the neck. "I love you, Alec," John said, barely audible.

"I love you, John," Alec responded into John's ear. With that, they both drifted off to sleep, John feeling safe and content in Alec's arms. And, for the first time in a while, Alec found himself relaxing. Maybe chaos wasn't so bad... as long as it came with good food and the right company.

The next morning, Alec awoke to sunlight making its way across the bed from the open window. He was alone. "So that was it?" He thought. "The story of my life. Good things don't last." The sadness that washed over him caused a single tear to fall on his cheek. How would he get past this? He was so sure that last night was something special.

Alec's fears were unfounded, however. He looked up to see John standing in the doorway, holding two steaming mugs of coffee. "I thought you might want some caffeine," John offered, extending one mug to Alec and then settling into the bed with the other. John nuzzled up next to Alec as he took a slow sip from the mug.

"This is nice," John mused, continuing to sip from the mug.

"Yes, John. It's so nice. I wonder if I'm dreaming."

"You're not dreaming, my friend."

"So, what happens now?" Alec asked.

"What do you want to happen?" John questioned back casually.

"Honestly?" Alec responded.

"Yes, of course. Let's agree to always be honest with each other, okay?" John shot back.

"Okay. Agreed," Alec responded. "My dream would be for this to continue. For us to be a couple. I feel like I could spend the rest of my life getting to know you. We would be great together, you know."

John sat quietly, sipping his coffee, deciding how to explain his emotional roller coaster to Alec.

"So," Alec continued, "I know this is happening quickly. We've been through a lot together as friends, and in a short time. But you wanted honesty, and that's it."

"Alec, this is sudden and new for me," John started.

Tears welled up in Alec's eyes. He knew what was coming. He couldn't talk, so he decided to drink his coffee and enjoy being with this man. The man that he loved. Any time with John was time that Alec would cherish.

"But," John finally continued, "I want to see where this goes. I do love you, Alec. And I can see myself spending the rest of my life with you. I'm not saying the transition will be easy. I just need for you to be patient with me. Are you okay with that?"

Alec placed his mug on the nightstand, grabbed John's, and did the same. He then leaned over and pulled John into him, hugging him tightly. "Yes, John. I'm okay with that. I'll take what I get. Let's see where this goes."

"I really want this, Alec. I've never felt this way about anyone. You are too important to me to not realize what we have. And how special that is!" John was overwhelmed with emotion as he hugged Alec back.

Alec moved his head from John's shoulder to face him. He pulled John close and kissed him passionately, tasting the coffee that had just been in John's mouth. "I love you, John. I'm going to tell you that every day, so get used to it."

Alec pushed John back on the bed and pulled down his shorts, revealing just how strong John's feelings were for him. Alec, who still had not put on any clothes from the evening before, straddled John, spit in his hand and reached behind him to ease himself down on John's throbbing, leaking cock. As they continued to make love, John took Alec's head in both hands and pulled him close to him, their eyes meeting. "I love you, Alec," John said definitively. "I want to be with you more than anything I've ever wanted." With that, they made love, exploring and learning. Once John was satisfied and had rested appropriately, Alec resting lightly on top of him, John said "Okay, now your turn."

"No, John. Sometimes, there are going to be times where it needs to be all about you. And that's okay. I just want to hold you. We can worry about me later. There are never any expectations with us. No obligations. I just want it to be about us being with each other. Okay?"

"Okay, Alec. I might need you to remind me of that from time to time. But you saying that makes me love you even more. If that's even possible!" John laughed.

"I'll remind you when you need reminding." Alec laughed with him. "For now, can we cuddle for a bit? I just want to hold you."

"I'll never turn down cuddle time with you!" John chuckled.

"What do you think our friends will say when they find out we're a couple?" John pondered.

"Our friends that know us will be happy for us. Some might even say it is about time this happened. Others who don't like it are not our problem," Alec replied casually.

John smiled at this. Alec was right, as usual. How could people not be happy for someone else's happiness?

"What's for lunch?" Alec queried.

"Have you ever tried my rice?" John retorted, laughing.

So they cuddled and talked, and planned, and laughed. They were content, happy lovers partners. And most importantly, friends.

The day had finally arrived for John and Alec to travel to the conference. As they sat at the airport gate, Alec reflected on the past three months. He and John had grown closer than he ever thought two people could. Although Alec initially resisted the feeling of dependence, he eventually accepted that he simply could not imagine life without John.

John had fully committed himself to their relationship and had never seen Alec so happy. When John's apartment lease was nearing its end, he casually suggested one morning that they move in together. They were lying in bed, having just finished an intense morning session of lovemaking, a ritual they both enjoyed to kickstart their day. Alec hesitated at first, afraid of relying too much on someone else, but he soon realized he couldn't envision a life without John by his side. Letting go of his past fears, he gave himself fully to their life together.

Alec had worried that combining their belongings would make his apartment feel overcrowded, but to his surprise, it worked. They managed to integrate their lives seamlessly with minimal stress. However, they both agreed that finding a larger place after the conference would be ideal, a home they could create and share as a couple.

The reaction from their friends had been positive. Most people wondered why they had not gotten together sooner. This was more difficult for John than for Alec. John never knew that people noticed how close his connection to Alec really was. In true John fashion, he accepted the comments, made a few sarcastic comments, and moved on with a smile and a laugh. Alec was simply content. More content than he had ever been. He embraced his new life with John in the true sense of the determinism in which he believed.

"I can't believe you upgraded us to First Class," John mused.

"It's a long flight. And we can afford it. Besides, you deserve the best!" Alec replied.

"I'm happy we're finally traveling together, Alec. It will be good to be with you in a different environment."

"Me too," Alec said.

"Do you mind if we go over the agenda again?" John asked. "I just want to make sure we have everything in place."

"Of course," Alec replied, smiling and leaning in towards John. He resisted the urge to kiss him, opting instead to lightly brush his fingers against John's leg. This casual and affectionate gesture in public always made John smile.

"You're purposefully distracting me, Alec," John said, still smiling.

"What? Me? I would never distract you with subversive public affection!" Alec laughed, his eyes bright and lively.

"Okay, Alec. I'm supposed to be the sarcastic one!" John grinned. "But you know I like it."

"Right. Okay, on to the schedule." Alec furrowed his brow and pursed his lips tightly in an effort to convey his seriousness.

John shook his head and laughed again. "So, after we pick up the rental car, we'll just make our way to the hotel. We need to get some food on the way. I'll be hungry."

"I suppose," Alec said, deep in thought. "We have some protein bars in my backpack. If I get too hangry, I'll have one of those."

"If you get too hangry, I'm going to leave you by the side of the road," John responded.

"You would never do that!" Alec exclaimed.

"No. But I can think about it!" John joked, laughing and casually moving his fingers along the side of Alec's leg.

"You need to stop that, John, or we're going to have to make a trip to the restroom together."

"You say that like I would say no," John said, trying to look serious, but his eyes belying his sarcasm.

"Now you've done it," Alec said. "I'm hard, and you're going to have to take care of it. Grab your bag and follow me."

Alec stood up abruptly, holding his backpack in front of him to hide the effect that John had on him. Always in public, he thought, laughing to himself.

John grabbed his bag and followed Alec. As they approached the restroom area, Alec noticed a family restroom and quickly went inside, followed by John. Before John could even lock the door, Alec had dropped his pants. John immediately knelt and took Alec's ample dick into his mouth, slowly sliding his lips along the shaft. Alec moaned loudly.

"Shhh," John said forcefully. "I know you like it, but you need to keep the noise down."

John continued as Alec used every bit of will power to stay quiet. It didn't take long.

"I'm coming," Alec whispered.

John continued, gripping Alec's shaft with his hand, his mouth continuing to work the head. Alec could not hold back, he released his load, and John took it all, swallowing quickly and continuing to suck and lick the cock that was all his.

"I can't believe you swallowed!" Alec exclaimed quietly.

"First time for everything," John replied. "You do it all the time with me, so I thought I'd give it a try."

"How was it?" Alec asked.

"Better than I thought it would be," John said. "I might just do it again!"

"Do you want me to take care of you?" Alec asked.

"No, I'm good. You can make it up to me at the hotel," John answered, leaning forward and kissing Alec hard on the lips.

Alec pulled up his pants and grabbed his backpack. John grabbed his bag and moved it in front of him to hide his erection as he exited the room. They walked back to the gate in silence, Alec walking slightly ahead of John, looking back every few minutes at John. Each time he had a grin of someone who had experienced supreme happiness.

Back at the gate, they settled in to wait for boarding, which was not for another 30 minutes. Alec leaned over to John and whispered quietly in his ear, "Thank you for that. I love you so much, John. And not just for things like this."

John smiled and replied, "I know, Alec. I know. I love you, too."

They boarded the plane and settled into their roomy seats for the 6-hour flight from Seattle to Miami. Alec had selected two joining seats in the center of the first-class cabin. There was a privacy panel that could be lowered for couples traveling together, as well as a sliding door to provide a small amount of privacy from the aisle. John lowered the privacy panel and reached a hand over to Alec. Alec grabbed his hand and squeezed tightly before letting go. The flight attendant arrived at John's seat with two glasses of champagne and small bowls of macadamia nuts. He was short and trim, his bright smile negated the seriousness initially portrayed by his close-cut dark hair and mustache.

"Good evening, gentlemen. I'm Nate, and I'll be taking care of you during the flight. Please don't hesitate to let me know if you need anything. The features of the seat are self-explanatory, and you two seem fairly competent, but let me know if you have questions." He smiled and winked at Alec, then smiled at John. "You two are such an attractive couple. And you seem so happy. We don't get much of that. Most couples are arguing by this point."

"Thanks, Nate," Alec responded. "We are happy." He looked at John and smiled.

"It shows," Nate said. "Anyway, the restrooms are up front. They are surprisingly roomy." His wink at Alec implied that he knew what Alec was thinking.

"Thanks," John replied, not entirely sure what was going on.

Alec had traveled first-class enough times to know how things worked, but this was John's first experience—both flying first-class and joining the mile-high club. They presented themselves as a happy couple, and Nate was determined to ensure they received extra attention during the flight. This would help discreetly shield their trip to the restroom from the notice of other passengers.

"What was that about?" John asked as Nate walked away to take care of other passengers.

"He's just telling us that he knows we're a couple, and he respects that we might want some private time in the restroom," Alec said quietly, winking at John. "And I think you might get some attention from me before we land, not after!"

"Wow, very assuming of you," John replied, his smile betraying his attempt at sarcasm.

"Alec know what John like," Alec replied in a caveman voice, making John burst out in laughter.

John raised his glass and clinked it with Alec's, "Here's to a good trip."

They started exploring the features of their first-class seats, munching on nuts, and sipping the cool, bubbly beverage. John was fascinated with the options available, particularly the small amenities bag. He put on the sleeping mask, sliding it up to his forehead, and opened everything in the pouch, sniffing and testing. With each object, he held it up to Alec and smiled before moving on to the next. He was like a kid with a new bag of toys. Alec watched him with true happiness in his heart. He felt so lucky to be with this man. The emotions often overwhelmed him, and he had to suppress them simply to function normally. Alec donned his noise-canceling headphones, sat back in his seat, closed his eyes, and waited for take-off. Nate came by to collect the nut dishes and empty glasses, being mindful to leave Alec undisturbed.

After take-off, Nate arrived at Alec's seat with two fresh beverages. "The restroom is free if you need it," he offered as he moved up to the front of the cabin.

"Shall we?" Alec looked at John as he unbuckled his seatbelt.

John grinned, unbuckled his seatbelt, and positioned his hands in front of him to hide what Alec's smile did to him. As they approached the first-class restroom, Nate opened the door and positioned himself so that it would be difficult for other passengers to see two men going in together. John entered first, followed by Alec. The restroom was larger than the typical aircraft restroom, not by much, but it was enough. Alec had flown once before on this particular type of aircraft and knew what to expect. At about twice the size of a typical aircraft lavatory, there was enough room for two people to comfortably stand without being too cramped. Alec followed John and quickly locked the door.

John quickly dropped his pants. Alec grabbed John firmly and kissed him deeply.

"Sit on the toilet lid," Alec commanded.

John closed the toilet lid and sat, without question, spreading his legs to give Alec access to the erection that had remained since Nate had given them the clear signal to use the washroom. Alec got on his knees, lightly stroking John's torso with his fingers. He then ran a single finger under John's balls, tracing the light hairy crease and continuing up the shaft of his penis, ending with a circular rub under the glans. John moaned and it was Alec's time to warn him about making too much noise.

"It's difficult keeping quiet with what you do to me," John whispered breathlessly.

"I know, my love," Alec said as he started kissing John's stomach. He knew John liked the feel of Alec's beard brushing against the skin of his belly.

Alec continued teasing John. Moving slowly between stroking his dick to licking the head, then kissing and tweaking his nipples. He fondled his balls until he felt them getting tight, knowing John was going to explode at any moment. Alec started moving his mouth slowly up and down John's shaft. Using the tip of his tongue to flick the sensitive area under the head with each movement. John could not hold back any longer, emptying a large load into Alec's warm mouth. Alec loved doing this to John. He loved the feeling of John's hot jizz hitting the back of his throat as he swallowed. He loved the way John's cock pulsed when he came. He loved pleasing John. He loved everything about this man.

John stood and pulled up his pants. As tucked in his shirt and buckled his belt, Alec raised the toilet lid to pee. When Alec finished urinating, he pulled John to him and kissed him gently. Alec's head ended up in the nape of John's neck, his favorite place. He kissed there softly and wrapped both arms around him, holding him tightly. John felt cared for, loved, needed, and wanted.

They unlocked the door to the restroom, exiting to see Nate working in the galley. He smiled at them with a sly wink and went back to his work. John and Alec made their way back to their seats and settled in, Alec opting to watch a movie while John explored the extensive variety of games available on the entertainment system. Nate arrived a few minutes later with a snack and more beverages. John had previously asked what kinds of whiskey they had on board and Nate had remembered. He presented two glasses of a top-shelf whiskey, neat, with a selection of crackers, cheese, and fruit.

"Just bringing snacks and drinks to get you settled. I'll be serving a meal in about an hour, and then you can take a nap if you like." Nate was brief and kind, delivering the drinks quickly and moving on to the row behind them.

"You doing okay?" Alec asked.

"I'm great, buddy," John replied, taking a sip of whiskey and popping a piece of cheese in his mouth. Alec loved when he called him buddy.

Alec returned to his movie, enjoying the whiskey and food.

The flight was long but pleasant. They ate, slept, watched movies, and occasionally chatted about a variety of things.

The plane landed uneventfully, and the two men were quiet on their walk to retrieve their luggage and rental car. After loading the luggage the rented SUV, Alec hopped in the driver's seat and familiarized himself with the controls while John connected his phone and started navigation to the hotel.

"Food?" John asked.

"Yes. Wanna be bad and stop at McDonald's?" Alec replied, his tone sheepish and hesitant, a big smile and raised eyebrows indicated that he expected the answer to be in the negative.

"That sounds good! I know it's bad for us, but I'll make sure we work it off later." John grinned at Alec, winked, and placed a hand on Alec's leg, allowing it to rest there as he searched for the fast-food restaurant on the map.

"Waypoint set. Drive on, my dear. Let's get some food."

Full bellies and a 20-minute drive brought them to the hotel. Alec checked in while John familiarized himself with the layout of the hotel and conference areas on a map in the lobby. Taking the elevator to the top floor, Alec was excited to see John's face when he realized that they had been upgraded to a full suite. John was over the top excited.

"Look at the view!" John exclaimed. "I can see the beach and the ocean and the city!"

"Only the best for you, babe," Alec responded, walking up behind John and wrapping his arms around him, nestling his chin on John's shoulder.

"You're definitely getting laid tonight!"

"Like that wasn't going to happen anyway!" Alec chuckled.

"Yeah, well, you might just get it more than once. Or twice." John turned his head and smirked at Alec. "Okay, so you would also get it more than once anyway. But I'm going to make it extra special."

"I don't know what that means, John. Sex with you is always extra special."

"I think you know what I mean, sweetheart. Don't be so coy," John teased.

"You... you mean you want to try bottoming?" Alec asked hesitantly. It was the one thing that John had resisted. He wanted to do it and had mentioned it a lot lately. Alec didn't want to push the issue. He wanted it to happen but knew that it would be a lot to take for someone's first time.

"Yep. I'm going to do it. I really want to do it. I'm just scared, Alec. You're so big, and I've never done it before. I don't want to fuck it up." John was thoughtful and wanted to please Alec.

"It's okay, my love. We will go slow," Alec reassured. "But first, you know what I need to do."

"Okay, okay, go unpack." Alec quipped. "But don't take all day." They had discussed this. One of Alec's many eccentricities involved a particular habit when traveling. Within minutes of being in a hotel, Alec liked to completely unpack. Everything either in drawers or on hangers. He had assured John that he could accomplish this task in a record-breaking 10 minutes.

John settled in one of the comfortable, easy chairs to watch the magic. And true to his work, Alec was done in under 10 minutes. John was very entertained watching Alec perform this task. He worked quickly and efficiently, unpacking all the clothes and even arranging the toiletries neatly on the bathroom counter. This strange habit only added to the connection that John felt for him.

"All done!" Alec proclaimed.

"That was truly impressive!" John said. "Now, take off your clothes and get on the bed." Alec's pants were down before John could even finish the command.

As Alec lay naked on the bed, John stood at the end of the bed and slowly undressed. Alec started to get up to help, but John pushed him back down.

"You get to watch, and I get to enjoy your body. No helping unless I say so.

Understood?" John was smiling, but Alec knew he was serious.

"Understood, Sir!" Alec yelled, bringing his hand up to his head in a crisp salute.

John continued to slowly remove his clothes. Teasing Alec by acting coy and turning away as he unzipped his pants. When he was completely naked, John started rubbing Alec's feet, occasionally allowing his erect penis to brush against his toes. Each time that happened, Alec uttered a guttural moan, followed by, "you're killing me, Johnny boy. I want to touch it so bad."

John didn't respond. He just kept teasing, moving slowly up Alec's body, exploring it like it was his first time. After 15 long minutes of rubbing and kissing various body parts, John had made his way up to Alec's face. They kissed slowly at first. John teasing Alec's mouth with his tongue before settling into the passionate kissing that had become a hallmark of their relationship.

John straddled Alec, positioning Alec's rock-hard massive cock between his ass cheeks. He let the pressure of his body apply pressure to Alec's cock, slowly grinding.

"You need to slow your roll, Johnny boy, or it's going to be over soon," Alec whispered.

"Shhh." John placed a single finger against Alec's lips as he stopped the movement of his hips. "What's your favorite position when you top?"

"I like to bottom face down. I like to feel the ass cheeks against my pelvis. I also get deeper that way," Alec said clinically. He was not sure John would agree to this.

John jumped up and flopped face down next to Alec. "Get on top, but go slow. Walk me through it. Please be gentle." John seemed willing but scared.

Alec positioned himself on top of John. He rested his hard cock in the crack to John's ass and softly kissed his neck. "Don't worry, my love. Just tell me if you need to stop."

Alec rolled to be to John's side, reached over to the bedside table, and grabbed the bottle of lube. He placed a little on his middle finger and placed his finger gently on John's ass, slowly moving the finger down to lube his hot hole.

"I'm going to play with your hole using my finger. I'll be gentle, and it will help loosen it up. I just want you to enjoy the sensation." Alec massaged John's sphincter with his finger, rubbing gently in a circular motion, occasionally applying pressure. John moaned with pleasure.

"The feeling is so intense. Go to the next step, please. I want you inside me," John whispered as Alec continued applying pressure.

"I'm going to apply more pressure. When I do, I want you to squeeze my finger with your sphincter. When I say squeeze, you squeeze. When I say release, you release. Understand?"

"Yes. Go slow." John acknowledged.

Alec applied some pressure and told John to squeeze, which he did. When Alec told him to release, Alec pushed his finger up to the second joint. His finger slid in easily. John moaned loudly and pushed his butt further onto Alec's finger.

"Fuck! Fuck! Fuck! That feels amazing. Keep going. Don't stop." John instructed with urgency.

Alec gently slid his finger in and out several times before pulling it out completely. He repositioned himself on top of John, adding more lube to both John's hole and his own cock, which was so hard by now that it felt like it was going to burst. He slid his big dick between John's crack and rested the tip against John's quivering hole. The hole that he had always wanted to take and was now ready and waiting for him. He applied a small amount of pressure and told John to squeeze. John squeezed and then immediately released, pushing himself fully on to Alec's throbbing cock. Alec was shocked that it went in all the way. That alone almost made him cum. John started rocking his hips, causing Alec's hard cock to slide in and out with each motion. Alec could tell that John's cock was rubbing against the sheets. He quickly reached under John and firmly grabbed his cock, allowing him to fuck his hand.

"I'm cumming!" John yelled.

"Me too!" Alec yelled.

"Oh my god, oh my god, oh my god," John screamed.

"Fuuuuck!" Alec screamed.

John couldn't catch his breath. His body heaved and trembled under Alec. Alec collapsed, exhausted, on top of John, then rolled to the side, his big cock pulling out of John's ass with an audible 'pop.'

They both suddenly laughed at the sound and turned to face each other. John grabbed Alec and pulled him close. They held each other tightly for several minutes, kissing and caressing each other.

"I can't believe how intense that was!" John said quietly.

"I know. It was for me, too," Alec admitted. "I've never been with anyone where we climaxed at the same time. That was amazing!"

John nuzzled his head on Alec's furry chest, quickly falling asleep. Alec fell asleep a few minutes later, reflecting on his supreme sense of contentment.

Alec woke an hour later. John had showered and was quietly reading the chair by the window.

"Hey," John said.

"Hey, babe," Alec said sleepily. "Come here."

John walked over to the bed and sat on the edge, he grabbed Alec's hand, bringing it to his lips and kissing each finger. Alec's hand rested on John's thigh.

"How do you feel?" Alec asked.

"A little sore and we definitely have to talk about going to the bathroom after getting fucked. That was interesting."

"Yeh, there's that. I should have warned you," Alec laughed.

"It was worth it, Alec. We are definitely doing that again! I feel closer to you than ever before."

"Ditto, my lover."

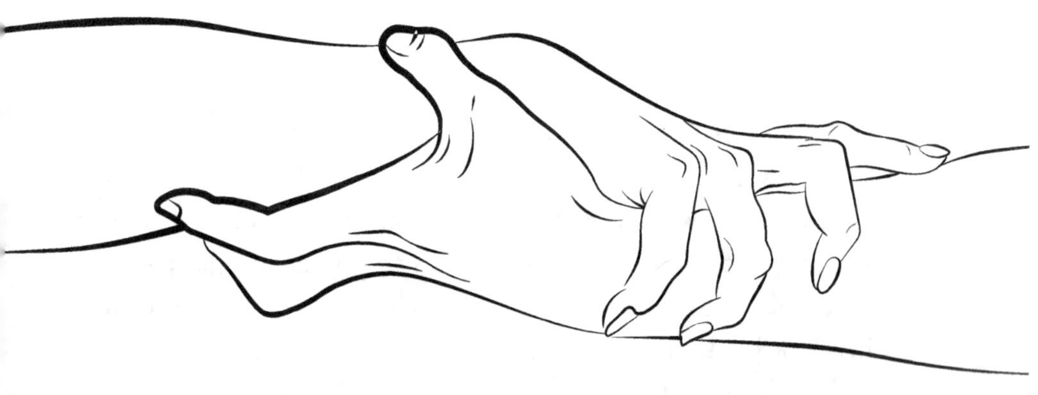

2: Second Spring

Greg and Grant, each stepping vibrantly through their fifties, discovered in each other a love that many only dream of. Their meeting was a serendipitous twist of fate, unfolding during a time of personal trials and transformations. Having each navigated the complexities of life – love lost, careers that took more than they gave, and the quiet loneliness of middle age – they found in one another in a second spring; a chance to rekindle dreams long thought extinguished.

Choosing love over all else, they embarked on a journey not just of the world but of the heart. Their first stop was Tokyo, where they nestled into a cozy hotel in Shiba Koen, a stone's throw from the lush, verdant gardens surrounding the Tokyo Tower. Their room, a harmonious blend of traditional Japanese aesthetics and modern comfort, became their sanctuary.

Each morning in Tokyo began the same way – with Greg softly

awakening in the tender embrace of Grant, their breaths synchronized, hearts beating in quiet anticipation of the day. Through their window, the city stretched endlessly, a tapestry of life and light that invited them to explore.

"Good morning, lover," Grant whispered softly in Greg's ear, his right hand sliding purposefully from its resting place on Greg's chest across the furry expanse of belly that had seen too many late-night ramen and not enough exercise. Grant's fingers gently played at the hair around Greg's belly button, occasionally brushing against the head of his rock-hard cock. Greg moaned softly with each touch. Grant turned his hand palm up and firmly grasped the shaft of Greg's thick uncut penis. It was only six inches in length but so thick that Grant's fingers barely met as he gently tugged. Grant's thumb slowly circled the mushroom head, greasing the foreskin with the Cowper's fluid leaking from the creases. He was always stunned at the amount of pre-cum Greg produced. So much so that they often needed no lube, a fact not lost on Grant as his hole twitched with the memory of the previous evening, still painful from being stretched further than he thought possible.

"Think you can take it again?" Greg chuckled, turning his face towards Grant, kissing him just below his right earlobe, a gesture that never ceased to cause a reaction.

"Oh yes," Grant replied, "I can take as many times as you can give it to me."

Without hesitation, Greg popped up to his knees and firmly flipped Grant onto his belly. Grant's ass immediately assumed a lordotic position, inviting Greg to enter at will. Greg retracted the foreskin from his slick head and gently placed the tip against Grant's quivering hole. With a movement that was smooth and quick, he slid his fat dick into Grant's warm, tight hole. Grant tensed and fought the intrusion, suddenly unsure if he could take it. He had this realization every time Greg fucked him. As Greg started slow strokes in and out, Grant relaxed and pushed back into Greg to get it as deep as possible. The pain was replaced with pleasure as Greg thrust faster and faster, his chest making full contact with Grant's back. Greg's right hand wrapped over Grant's right shoulder and under his neck, pulling his head back. Greg's left hand deftly made its way along Grant's hip and under his body to grab his cock. Greg loved Grant's cock – all 9 inches of it. It wasn't very thick, but Greg still found it challenging to take it when Grant fucked him. Fortunately, Grant liked to bottom more than top, but on occasion, Greg would give it up and let Grant fuck him. However they did it, sex was always the best either of them had ever had.

Continuing toward the goal, Greg's strokes became faster. "You want this load, baby?" Greg whispered in Grant's ear, his breath short from the exertion of this final push.

"Give it to me," Grant responded. "I want it all. Drop your load in me. I need every last drop."

With that statement, Greg unloaded in Grant's ass, continuing to pump until every last bit was deposited. Exhausted, he collapsed on Grant's back, his fingers softly playing with Grant's tousled salt and pepper hair. "I love you so much," he whispered in Grant's ear. "Now turn over and let me suck you off. I need some nourishment after that. Your tight ass always makes me cum so hard!"

Grant rolled onto his back as Greg quickly pulled his cock out of Grant's ass, the remaining cum dripping from the foreskin. He positioned himself on Grant's left side and kissed Grant gently on the lips, pressing harder as his fingers found Grant's right nipple. He pinched the nipple with this thumb and forefinger, eliciting a moan from Grant.

"You know all my spots, babe," Grant said breathlessly.

"Yep, and I'm going to make my way to all of them," Greg replied, kissing Grant's neck in a line from his throat to just under his earlobe. Grant's reaction was exactly what Greg wanted, as he writhed under his affection.

Greg's hand moved quickly across Grant's smooth torso until he found Grant's rock-hard cock. Pausing only briefly on his erect member, Greg let his fingers trace a line from the head, down the shaft, and continuing along the centerline of his balls until he reached that sensitive area between his scrotum and his hole. Greg's fingers gently stroked Grant's hole, still sloppy with jizz. Grant's moans because loader, his hard cock twitching and flexing as Greg's fingers made circles around his cum-wet anus.

"Fuck, I feel like I'm going to cum, and you're not even touching my dick," Grant exclaimed.

Greg moved his head down to Grant's throbbing cock, continuing the gentle stokes around his hole. Greg put his lips on the head of Grant's cock and slowly pulled it into his mouth. That was all it took. Grant exploded in Greg's mouth. Greg kept it in as deep as he could, feeling Grant's hot jizz hit the back of his throat. This was Greg's favorite thing. He loved the sensation of the warm fluid filling his mouth and trickling down the back of his throat. As much as he liked fucking, he could to this every day and be perfectly happy. Feeling Grant's reaction to his touch gave him satisfaction like no other.

"That was a nice breakfast!" Greg said. "But I'm going to need something else. Let's wash up and go out for a walk."

They made their way to the large walk-in shower, jizz dripping from Grant's limp cock as he walked across the room.

"Looks like I missed some," Greg said as he squatted in front of Grant and licked the fluid from the tip of his dick. He stood up quickly and kissed Grant deeply. Grant could taste his own cum on Greg's tongue, his erection returning immediately.

"What's this?" Greg laughed, gently stroking Grant's erection.

"That, babe, is what you do to me," Grant answered, giving

Greg a quick kiss on the neck. "But this one can wait. Let's clean up. I'm hungry, too."

After showering and getting dressed, they ambled through the vibrant streets, hand in hand, finding solace in the simple joys of life. Breakfast had become a sacred ritual as they sought out the best ramen shops, their laughs and chatter mingling with the steam rising from bowls of rich, flavorful broth and perfectly cooked noodles.

The afternoon was spent meandering among the solemn beauty of Shinto shrines, their spirits touched by the tranquility and timeless wisdom that seemed to permeate the air. They found peace in the simple acts of washing their hands and mouth at the temizuya and in the gentle clapping of hands and bowing before the kami.

The next chapter of their journey unfolded in Shanghai. Their accommodation, a high-rise hotel in the bustling heart of the city, offered a stark contrast to the quaint charm of Tokyo. Here, mornings were greeted with the same tender closeness, their shared gaze now lingering over the sprawling urban landscape of Shanghai after an intense session of love-making.

This particular morning, Grant wanted to top. Greg found unexpected pleasure in his face being pressed against the floor-to-ceiling window as Grant pounded him from behind. Grant's cock always slid in easily, but the length made Greg gasp and catch his breath as Grant's full nine inches penetrated all the way into his tight hole. Greg loved feeling Grant's balls slap against him with each thrust. When Grant came inside him, the moment felt like they had become one person. Grant was not verbal when he fucked Greg. But he did like to bite. Greg's shoulders and back would maintain teeth marks for hours afterward. This also was an unexpected pleasure for Greg. New experiences were one of the things Greg loved most about being with Grant.

Greg, with his funny attempts at speaking Mandarin, navigated the vibrant streets of the city with a careless ease, his love for Grant shining in his eyes with each translated phrase and shared story. They lost themselves in the bustling markets, savored the rich flavors of street food, and marveled at the juxtaposition of ancient temples against the backdrop of soaring skyscrapers.

Evenings in Shanghai found them in quiet contemplation, often speaking of future destinations – Paris, perhaps, or maybe a serene retreat in the Icelandic countryside. Where would they enjoy each other's bodies next? Yet, their conversations always circled back to the present, to the incredible fortune of having found each other, of having a second chance at love.

Greg and Grant, in each other's arms, realized that this journey was more than just a physical trek across continents. It was more than intense sex. It was a testament to the enduring power of love, the kind that comes softly but grows fervently, flourishing against all odds. In their twilight years, they found not just a companion but a soulmate in each other.

Their story, unfolding one city at a time, was a reminder that love, indeed, knows no age or boundaries. In their shared smiles, gentle touches, and in the quiet certainty of their presence together, they celebrated this unexpected yet profoundly beautiful chapter of their lives. In every sunrise viewed from different corners of the world, in every shared adventure and whispered word of love, Greg and Grant cherished their unique bond, a love that was truly their own – timeless and untamed by the passing years.

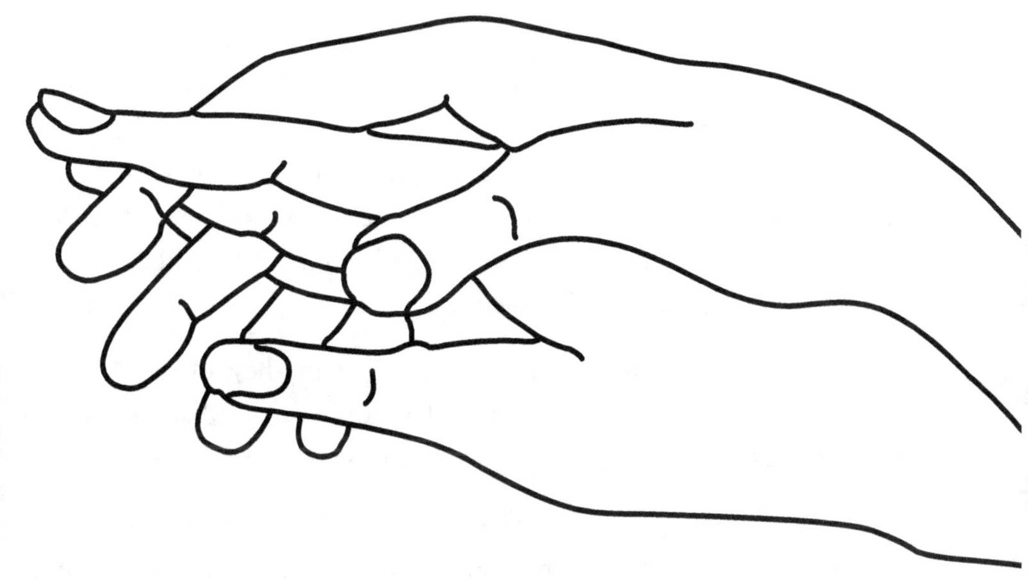

3: The Man on the Park Bench

Every morning, when I embarked on my routine morning run through the tranquil city park, I couldn't help but notice him. A man, roughly in his forties, lay sprawled across a park bench, his rugged appearance contrasting sharply with the sleek, expensive triathlon bike that rested beside him. It was a peculiar sight, one that never ceased to intrigue me.

The first time I saw him, I had assumed that perhaps he was a dedicated athlete who had fallen on hard times. His triathlon bike was a testament to his commitment to the sport, its carbon frame and aerodynamic design showcasing a level of passion and investment that was undeniable. It was as though his dreams and aspirations had collided with the harsh reality of life on the streets.

As the weeks went by, I found myself looking forward to my encounters with the enigmatic man on the park bench. I noticed the little details that painted a more complex picture of his life. Despite his disheveled appearance, his grooming was impeccable. His hair was neatly trimmed, his beard carefully maintained, and his clothes, though worn, were always clean. It was as though he clung to a semblance of normalcy amid the chaos of homelessness.

One cool autumn morning, curiosity got the best of me, and I decided to strike up a conversation. I slowed my pace and approached him cautiously. "Morning," I greeted him with a nod and a friendly smile.

He looked up from his makeshift bed, his eyes betraying a sense of surprise. "Morning," he replied, his voice tinged with a hint of uncertainty.

I gestured toward his triathlon bike. "That's a beautiful bike you have there. Are you a triathlete?"

His face softened as he glanced at the bike, a mixture of pride and sorrow in his eyes. "Yeah, used to be. Trained for years, even competed in a few Ironman events."

I was taken aback. "So, what happened? Why are you here?"

He sighed, a heavy burden clearly weighing on his shoulders. "Life took a few unexpected turns. Lost my job, had some family issues, and before I knew it, I ended up here. The bike... it's all I have left of my old life."

As he spoke, I realized that beneath the layers of hardship and misfortune, there was a man with a story—a story of determination, passion, and resilience. He had fallen, but he hadn't given up on his dreams entirely.

"I'm Justin," I offered, extending a hand in greeting.

"Michael," he returned, shaking my hand with the position and pressure of someone who had been trained in business etiquette.

"Will you be here tomorrow?" I asked.

"Probably," he answered.

"Cool. I'll see you tomorrow," I stated. "Michael. . . forgive me for asking, but do you have enough food?"

"No worries, Justin. It's a fair question. I do have enough food. I have a job, just no place to live." His voice portrayed confidence but was tinged with sadness.

"That's good. Still, I might bring us some breakfast burritos tomorrow. Is that okay? There's a food truck near my house that has some really good ones. Any food allergies?" I was rambling.

"No, I eat anything. Always have," he chuckled. "But yeah, that would be nice."

"Coffee? Cream, sugar, black?" I continued.

"Just black, please," Michael replied.

"Sounds good, my new friend. I'll see you tomorrow." I waived as I continued my run.

The next morning, I grabbed two burritos and two black coffees from the food truck and jogged the short distance to the park. Working from home as a tech advisor for a large healthcare company had its advantages. I enjoyed my slow mornings, going for a run, grabbing breakfast, and meeting new people. So, this morning, I did not feel rushed as I juggled the two coffees and a small bag with the food. As I approached, I could see that Michael was sitting on the park bench waiting. His backpack was packed, and his belongings stacked neatly beside his bike.

"Good morning, Justin!" His smile was disarming. I did not realize until that moment how attractive he was.

"Good morning!" I replied, extending a burrito while struggling to balance the two coffees. "Bacon, egg, and cheese. Not the healthiest, but I figured it was appropriate for our first breakfast together."

"It's perfect. My favorite. Thank you," he replied.

I sat down next to him on the bench, and we ate in silence. Enjoying the crisp air and watching people walk by. He finished his burrito quickly and sipped the hot coffee.

"Justin, you said this was our first breakfast. Do you intend for there to be others?" His question was tentative, filled with hope, expecting to be disappointed at the answer.

"I hope there will be others. I don't want you to think of this as charity. I just think you are an interesting guy, and I want to get to know you better." I immediately regretted my reply. Charity was exactly what bringing a homeless man a burrito was. "I'm sorry, that came out wrong."

"You're funny," he laughed. "I'm homeless, and you brought me food. That looks like charity to me. But it's okay. I didn't need you to bring me food. We established that up front. Let's pretend like I'm not homeless. That might make it easier."

"Deal," I said. But in the back of my mind, I knew the fact that he was homeless would be something that I would have to be okay with.

"You're a very attractive man," I said. "Hope you don't mind that I tell you that."

"Thanks. Don't mind at all. You're not so bad yourself." He smiled at me.

That smile gave me an immediate erection. I shifted my coffee to try to hide it, but hiding an erection in running shorts is impossible.

"It's a bit chilly. Do you mind if I get my blanket out?" he asked.

"Not at all," I replied.

Michael reached into one of his bags and pulled out a heavy, clean blanket. The pattern was a southwest motif in shades of gray. He draped the blanket across us, moving closer to me in the process.

"This okay?" he asked.

"Yes," I responded, my nervousness coming through in my answer.

Michael had placed his coffee on the ground, leaving both hands free. His left hand made its way to my knee under the blanket. I jerked slightly at his touch. My already rock-hard cock twitched at his hand on my knee. He continued to look straight ahead as his hand brushed against my erection. His fingers hooked under my shorts, their three-inch inseam giving him easy access. His warm hand grabbed my cock and slowly started to stroke it. Gently at first and becoming more urgent as his grip massaged the head. The feeling was intoxicating, and I came quickly with an intensity that I had not experienced in a long time.

He pulled his hand back, raised it to his lips, and licked it clean, turning his head to face me, grinning. He gave me a sly wink. "Is that what you wanted?" he asked.

"Yes. That was amazing. I feel like I need to return the favor." My reply was hesitant. I had no idea what to do in this situation.

"You'll have your chance," he replied. "See you tomorrow?"

"Yes." And with my reply, I stood up and walked back home. No run today. I needed to process what had just happened.

The next morning, I showed up at the park bench without running clothes. Dressed in jeans and a light hoodie, I approached the park bench to see Michael waiting with two coffees and two donuts.

"My turn for breakfast," he said.

"Thanks, do you mind if we walk while we eat? I want you to come back to my apartment with me." I still don't know why I trusted him enough to bring him home. Something about his gentle nature just seemed okay to me.

"Uh, okay. Are you sure, Justin?" You don't have to do that." I'm sure he was having thoughts of how to recognize a serial killer.

"Yes, I can't get you out of my mind, and I need to get to know you better."

We walked slowly back to my apartment. Me pushing his bike while holding a coffee and donut in one hand, nibbling on the pastry, and sipping the coffee with skill that surprised even me.

"So, Justin, what do you want to know about me?" Michael could sense that I wanted to know more of his story.

"Just tell me something about yourself, Michael. Anything, I just want to get to know you better."

"Okay, well, I'm an accountant. I had a bad turn of events that caused me to lose everything. But I was able to keep my bike and that makes me happy. The details of that story are better for telling over a drink. For now, I have a job as a bookkeeper. My co-workers do not know that I'm homeless. I have gym membership at a cheap gym nearby, and I shower there before work. I also sometimes get in a workout in the evenings. I vary where I sleep, depending on being asked by the cops to move. How's that for a start?"

"It's more than I expected. Thank you for sharing that with me."

By this point, we had arrived at my apartment building, and we made our way in the elevator to my small one-bedroom apartment on the 18th floor. As soon as the door closed and I had carefully placed his bike against the wall, I pushed him against the closed door and kissed him with a passion that had been building since the previous morning. He responded, his tongue exploring my mouth with an urgency that made my cock rock hard once again.

His hands rested on my hips and pulled me forcefully into him. I could feel his erection through his pants. He pushed me away slightly and grabbed my shoulders. "I haven't showered since yesterday morning, so maybe we can start there?" his concern evident in his tone.

"I would like that," I replied.

I took his hand and guided him towards my bathroom. I turned on the water in the shower and waited for it to get hot. Michael pulled his shirt over his head, revealing a body that was trim and toned. His chest was covered in a light dusting of dark brown hair, extending down across his six-pack abs and into the waistband of his pants. Not able to wait, I moved forward and unbuttoned his khakis, pushing them down to his thighs, along with his underwear. His ample erect cock sprang free. It was a perfect seven inches, with a slight curve upwards and a beautiful large, well-proportioned head. I wrapped my hand around it and tugged gently. He pushed me away and looked me up and down.

"Take off your clothes," he commanded as he stepped into the shower, looking back at me with that smile that almost made me cum in my pants.

I undressed quickly and joined him in the shower, where he had already lathered up. He moved me into the stream of water and started washing me with the bar of soap. He moved close to me so that our cocks brushed together, leaning forward to kiss me. His tongue once again exploring, probing. I reached for his hard cock, but he brushed my hand away, teasing me, continuing the passionate kiss.

We continued this foreplay while rinsing off. And while drying off. He was definitely a master at building anticipation. We moved to the bed, both naked and still damp from showering. Michael pushed me back on the bed, spread my legs, and positioned himself on his knees between my thighs. He gently stroked my smooth torso with both hands, ending at my balls, which he gently cupped and stroked. Grabbing my super hard, thick, 8-inch cock at the base, he sucked lightly at the head, swirling his tongue around the ridge of the head, then moving his warm mouth slowly down the shaft and back up again.

He extended himself to be entirely on top of me, mirroring my body, his head resting lightly in the nape of my neck.

"I'm going to ride your thick cock so hard," he whispered in my ear, grinding himself against me.

"I'm going to fuck you so hard," I responded, not sure how long I would last with the edging he had already given me.

Michael pulled his knees up alongside my hips and positioned his firm ass crack directly on my throbbing dick. He reached over to the nightstand and grabbed the bottle of lube that I had staged there. He continued to press his ass into my cock. I could feel the heat of his waiting hole. He squeezed a bit of lube into his hand and reached back to where my cock connected with his ass. His lubed fingers slid between the two, greasing the way for what was coming.

He leaned forward and kissed me with the same passion as he had in the shower. As he leaned forward, my hard cock slid up the back of his ass crack. As he pushed back, the fat head of my cock entered his waiting hole. It was tight. Oh, so tight.

"It's been a while," he whispered. "I need to take it slow."

"Take all the time you need, though I'm not sure how long I'll last once you get it in. You got me so worked up!" I responded.

"That's the idea," he laughed.

He slowly lowered himself onto my cock. Teasing the head slowly until his hole opened enough to accommodate the girth. This had been a problem with guys in the past, some not even willing to try once they saw it. Michael was different. He was going to take it like a champ.

After a bit of teasing his hole, I gave a single slow push-up and entered him fully. He gasped with a deep intake of breath, then pushed me in even further. He moaned as he ground down on my cock. I couldn't believe he could take it all. His hips rocked back and forward. It would not take long if he kept this up.

"Slow down, slow down," I said, my breath catching between each word.

He smiled and stopped all movement, reaching down to stroke my chest, then reaching one hand back to tickle my balls.

"Stop that!" I laughed as I grabbed his cock and started to stroke it.

As I stroked his hard cock, he started back milking my dick. I could feel his balls tighten as he approached orgasm. With a long groan, he unloaded on my stomach and chest, parts of the jizz stream reaching as far as my neck. The throb of his orgasm took me over the edge. I unloaded in his hot hole as he kept rocking, milking my huge dick to get all he could. After my body stopped shaking, he dismounted and laid down beside me, his hand resting gently on my stomach, his fingers playing with the remnants of his own jizz. Exhausted, our heads turned toward each other. He smiled. That smile. I leaned forward and kissed him gently on the lips, then returned to face the ceiling.

"I could get used to this," I said.

"I know, but we need to be practical about things, Justin. You don't really know me." His response was timid and hopeful.

"I want to get to know you. Let's talk about how to make that work." My response was genuine.

We both called out sick from work, and Michael spent the day with me. We made lunch, had two more sessions of mind-blowing sex, and got to know each other. He stayed the night as well. I learned that sometimes good people are simply in bad places and need someone to give them a chance. That was two years ago, and he's still here.

4: The Guy at the Yoga Studio

The parking lot was mostly full as I slowly drove up and down the aisles, trying to find an available space. Who designed these things? There were at least 20 businesses in the strip mall and parking for no more than 10, if that. This was my first time at this yoga studio. My officemates had given me a gift certificate for my birthday last month, knowing that I had been trying different studios around town. I had moved into the city ten months ago and had hoped to find a studio where I could be a regular, hone my skills, and possibly make new friends. So far, that had not happened. The only thing I had found were bitchy women who used the idea of yoga as a forum to gossip and meet before going out for drinks. But maybe this would be the one.

"Finally!" I exclaimed as an available spot finally presented itself. I backed my truck into the spot and grabbed my water bottle and towel before exiting the truck. The walk to the yoga studio was short, and I noticed a few looks along the way. At almost six feet tall, with a shaved head and a substantial beard, I frequently garnered looks from others—especially from other gay men and women who fantasized about them. Of course, the tight compression shirt and three-inch inseam shorts didn't hurt. My hairy muscular legs enhanced the obvious bulge that left nothing to the imagination concerning what was in my shorts. Certain God-given anatomy can't be helped. Even in my 40's, my body was the envy of much younger guys. I took pride in my health, focusing on moderation with what I ate, and included regular practice of running, swimming, and yoga. I had tried to include biking in my routine, but just never took to it.

As I entered the small ante room to the studio, I was greeted by a chipper blond woman sitting behind a small service counter. Ann was in her 50s and had the body of an 18-year-old. Yoga had clearly been good for her. Lavender and cedar lightly scented the air.

"Good afternoon! You must be Kevin. I'm Ann. This is my studio. I'm so glad you made it today." Ann was chipper in a nice and non-annoying way.

"Good afternoon," I responded. "Is parking always this difficult?" I immediately regretted starting the conversation with negativity.

"No, this is unusual. The store down the way is having a going-out-of-business sale, and it's been this way all week. Fortunately, they are closing for good tomorrow." Ann's positivity rubbed off on me.

"Sorry for being so negative," I interjected. "I think I really need this class today."

"It's okay," Ann responded. "We all have those moments. It will be a good class today. Only six people, so we can spread out. I'll also allow for some time at the end for you to remain in shavasana for a bit. Use that time to re-center and relax."

"Sounds wonderful." I breathed out a sigh of relief.

When I entered the studio, there were already four women on their mats, each sitting with their legs crossed, quietly keeping to themselves and preparing for class. "This might not be so bad," I thought to myself. I grabbed a mat and two cork blocks, found a space at the back of the room, and settled into a comfortable position to prepare my mind and body for the class. The room was warm but not hot, and soft amber lighting added to the ambiance to create a space that was both comfortable and intimate. It reminded me of my favorite studio in the suburbs where I used to live.

Ann entered the room and stood on a mat at the front of the room. The mirrored wall in front of her allowed me to see everyone in the room, as well as the door to the lobby. Ann started her introduction and was interrupted when the door opened. A man stood in the doorway, only his silhouette visible in front of the light from the other room.

"Sorry, am I late?" the guy said.

"No at all, we're just getting started. You must be Tom," Ann said kindly. "And we don't say sorry in this room. This is a place for healing and peace. Grab a mat and a couple of blocks, Tom. There's a place in the back next to Kevin."

As Tom approached my general direction, I could see that he was strikingly handsome. At maybe 5'9", he was shorter than the guys I usually dated. But boy, was he good-looking. Mostly hairless, with a light dusting of brown hair peeking out from his low-cut tank top. His shorts revealed muscular legs and a decent package that left me wanting to know what was in them. His chiseled jaw and tousled light brown hair perfectly complimented a brilliant and genuinely friendly smile. My pulse quickened. I didn't even know if he was gay. He might have a wife and four kids. I smiled back and nervously patted the floor beside me.

"Welcome," I said awkwardly. "I'm Kevin, but I guess you already know that. And you're Tom. Welcome." I was rambling.

"Hi, Kevin. Mind if I take up this spot?"

"Please do. Have you been here before?

"No. First time. Gift certificate from friends."

"Me too! Well, from co-workers."

"Cool. Let's check in after and compare notes."

"Sounds good."

"Okay, everyone, let's get started," Ann interrupted, clearly ready to get the class started.

The class was good. The flow was good. I tried hard not to look at Tom. But every time I looked over at him, he was looking back at me. I hoped I wasn't misinterpreting the situation.

At the end of class, as promised, Ann instructed us all to take the position of Shavasana. On our backs, prone, with hands positioned comfortably away from our bodies, I focused on my breath. In and out through the nose. The lights dimmed even more, and the music softly ended as Ann started sounding the quartz singing bowls. The sound radiated around the room, adding to the relaxing environment. Suddenly, I felt something touch my pinkie finger. Was that Tom? I slowly turned my head to the right and saw him looking right at me. In the dim light, I could barely make out his face. His bright smile was clear, however, as his finger slowly wrapped around mine. My heart beat faster. What was happening? I had experienced unexpected hook ups before, but never with this level of intimacy. We stayed in this position for what seemed like a very long time.

As the lights came back up and the sound of the bowls diminished, Ann offered parting words of wisdom about something. I wasn't paying attention. My thoughts raced at what had just happened. What did this mean? He was clearly interested, but all I knew about him was that he was good-looking, and his name is Tom.

"Namaste," Ann said.

"Namaste," the class responded in unison.

I sat up and pulled my knees to my chest for a moment of reflection.

Tom stood up, placed his blocks on the shelf in the corner, and neatly put his mat away. Then he exited the room. So that was it. He teases me then leaves. What a jerk. I mopingly put away the blocks and mat. This is what my luck with guys looked like. Promises of things not delivered.

I exited the room, my head low, my gaze towards the floor. Ann was waiting in the lobby.

"What did you think?" she asked.

"Um, I like it," I replied. "I think I'd like to give this place a try." My mind secretly hoping that maybe Tom would do the same. At least I could confront him about being such a tease.

I walked out the door and turned right towards the area where my truck was parked.

"What took you so long?" a voice called from behind me.

I turned around to see Tom. He stepped closer and gently placed a hand on my arm. "I didn't think you'd ever finish in there."

"I thought you had left," I replied.

"No, I told you I wanted to compare notes, I just didn't want to do it in there." His smile immediately melted any doubt I had. "Let's walk to your car." Tom motioned with his hand, indicating that I was to lead the way.

"Sounds good. So what did you think?" I asked.

"I really liked it. I think I'm going to give it a try. I've had a hard time finding a studio to call home. How about you?"

"I like it. I've had the same challenge. But I really like this place. Plus, there seems to be an added benefit." I winked at him as he chuckled at my comment.

We arrived at my truck, and Tom because immediately fascinated by the vehicle itself. "Is this all electric?" He asked.

"Yeah, all-electric. There's storage where the engine would normally be, and the back seat is huge!" I replied.

"Let me see," Tom remarked as he opened the back door and climbed inside. "Come on in!" His laugh was infectious. I smiled and got into the back seat with him.

"This is comfy!" Tom said as he scooted across the big back seat to make room for me to get in and close the door.

Then Tom turned towards and just looked at me.

"Listen, I'm not sure if was misreading you in there, but I really liked you touching my finger like that." I decided to be direct with him. "Oh, and I also tend to be direct. Fair warning."

"I like direct, Kevin. And you were not misreading my intentions. I don't usually do that sort of thing. But when you said hello and smiled at me, I felt a connection that I usually don't get with guys. Did you feel it, too?" Tom's query ended with a timid tone that made me think he was suddenly questioning if he had misread the situation.

"No, Tom, you are absolutely right. I felt it, too."

Without hesitation, he leaned forward and kissed me gently on the lips. I reciprocated, and he pressed harder. His tongue found mine, releasing passion that had been building during the yoga class. My hand found its way to Tom's stomach, and I reached under his tank top, placing my palm firmly on his belly. The hair there was light and soft. I ran my hand slowly up to his chest, where the hair was thicker. He moaned as my finger brushed a hard nipple and my tongue propped further into his wet mouth.

Tom's hand went directly for my crotch, massaging my massive erection. He pulled away and looked at me, his hand remaining in place.

"I was hoping it was as big as it looked in your shorts," he whispered.

"I've been told it's above average," I said, smiling.

"Well, mine's average, at best. So don't be disappointed when you see it," Tom said sheepishly.

"That's good," I said. "I like them on the average side."

He moved closer to me, gave me a quick but deep kiss, and moved both hands down to my shorts. Hooking his fingers into the waistband, he pulled them down slowly.

"I really, really want to see it."

"It's all yours," I said, motioning to my crotch.

Tom freed my big erect dick from my shorts. It popped up as it came out of the waistband, standing at its full 9 inches of attention.

"My god!" He exclaimed. "It's huge!" He took my ample head into his mouth gently at first, getting it wet with saliva before sliding his lips all the way down the shaft.

"Not many guys that can do that!" I remarked.

Tom ignored me as he continued to enjoy my dick. He worked every inch of it. The pleasure was unlike anything I had experienced. This guy really knew what he was doing. After a few minutes of bliss, I pulled his head up. "Kiss me," I demanded softly. His mouth met mine, and I could taste myself on his lips. "I want a go at yours," I said.

I knelt sideways by the seat and instructed him to lie down. He kicked off his shoes and bent his knees to comply. I shimmied his shorts down as he pulled his shirt off. His cock was perfect. Six inches, symmetrical, with a large head and a slight curve upwards. After getting his shorts completely off, I softly kissed his belly, my beard brushing against his erection. Pulling back, I gently traced a line with my finger from his tight balls, up his shaft, and around the head of his beautiful cock. His groans told me that I was doing it right. Hovering my head a few inches above his crotch, I let some spit fall directly onto the head, massaging it in with my tongue, performing an acrobat of circles and loops on the underside of his glans. His groans and moans intensified.

"You're going to make me cum!" he said, his breath short and quick.

"Good," I replied.

My mouth took in his entire dick. I slid it down, then up, and rested at the head. My tongue worked the underside of his head until I could feel his balls tighten. He was ready to shoot. When I felt his cock stiffen more than I thought it could, I slid my mouth all the way down. His orgasm was intense. I could feel the jizz hit the back of my throat. He came and came. I didn't think he would stop. When the pulsing of his erection slowed, his entire body collapsed, his one hand falling to the floor of the truck, then reaching up to gently caress my head.

"That was so intense, Kevin. I've never had an orgasm like that. And I've had many."

I withdrew my mouth and licked up the few remaining drops that oozed from his softening cock. I rested my head on his belly, my face towards his feet, and softly stroked his legs. We stayed that way in silence while he recovered. After a few minutes, Tom abruptly sat up. "My turn," he said.

I was not going to argue.

"Sit in the seat," he directed. And I did.

He pulled off my shirt and started running his hand through the thick hair on my chest.

"I love your fur," he said as he learned forward to kiss me.

Tom continued to rub my chest and belly, his lips never breaking contact with mine. Gradually, his hand found its way to my balls, circumnavigating my throbbing erection. This guy really was a tease! His fingers played lightly with the underside of my balls before moving slowly up to my long, thick shaft. His hand wrapped around it with a loose firmness, moving up and down slowly. Occasionally, the ridge of his fingers would catch the rim of my head and send electricity through my body.

His lips never left mine. His kisses cycled from soft to hard, matching the motions of his hand. He brought me slowly. When I did come, it was prolonged. The build-up lasted several minutes, and the actual orgasm wracked my body. His lips maintained constant contact with mine. My breath quickened as I shot my load on my belly. Only then did his lips leave mine. His hand pulled up, catching the remaining cum. His eyes stared into mine. I could not pull my gaze away. He raised his hand to his lips and slowly licked the cum from his fingers. His enjoyment was methodical and deliberate. His enjoyment at this immense.

As Tom settled into the seat beside me, we both sat quietly for a few minutes. "Want to get some dinner?" I asked.

"Yes," Tom replied eagerly.

"I like where this is going," I said.

"Me too, Kevin. You're different. In a good way," he smiled.

That smile. It still makes me weak. That was 10 years ago. That one yoga class. From a gift certificate given by co-workers. That one yoga class. The one that changed my life for the better.

5: Parole

Corey sat at the table in the prison library, immersed in the book of short stories that he had picked off the shelf to pass the time. The tan block walls and industrial tile flooring were at odds with the mahogany table and leather wingback chairs that had been donated by a local socialite in an effort to charitably improve the lives of those incarcerated. Corey liked the chairs. He couldn't care less about the fancy table. But the chair was super comfortable.

"Inmate." The guard stood over Corey, demanding his attention. "You have a visitor."

Silently, Corey stood, his gaze to the floor, and shuffled after the guard. They exited the library and turned left in the hallway towards the area that housed the visitation booths. The guard scanned his badge and opened the door to a large room with rows of partitions against the other three walls. Typical of older prisons, each partitioned booth involved a reinforced glass window framed by an old-style telephone to one side. The scene was mirrored on the opposite side of the glass, where each visitor would sit and communicate with their prisoner.

Corey immediately saw Jason sitting at one of the booths to the left. Jason smiled as soon as he saw Corey walk through the door. Corey's whole body melted at that smile. This was their third in-person visit, although they had been corresponding for almost two years. Corey wasn't expecting to see him today, and his heart was full of joy at seeing Jason's smiling face. Jason was already holding the phone up to his ear, so Corey rushed over and picked up the phone on his side.

"Hey, Buddy!" Jason said. "I thought I'd take the chance and see if they would let me see you. You must have been a good boy this week."

"I'm so happy. I don't even know what to say. I didn't know when I would see you next," Corey replied.

"I have to travel for work, so it might be a couple of months before I can come back and I just really needed to see you." Jason's voice was emotional. "How are you?"

"I'm really good. My parole hearing is coming up next week. Fingers crossed." Corey sounded nervous. What happened if he didn't get paroled? He had been in for just over 20 years. Maybe staying in was better. The world had changed so much. At this point, however, Jason was the sole reason that he wanted out.

"That's great, buddy! I'll be sending all my best good vibes your way," Jason said, sounding hopeful.

"Well, it's a long shot, but you never know," Corey mumbled. "Enough about me, what's going on with you?

"Same old thing," Jason responded. "My wife is busy with the kids, and work is busy. But it's all good. Afterall, I'm sitting here talking to you, so life is good."

"Inmate, 2-minute warning." The guard stood over Corey's shoulder, waiting for him to finish.

"Some privacy, please!" Corey looked back at the guard, who just looked at Corey and didn't move. "Okay, my friend," Corey looked at Jason, "I'll keep you updated through the app. We need to talk about what happens if I get out."

"Sounds good, buddy." Corey loved it when Jason called him "buddy." It made him feel wanted, needed, loved, adored, calm, excited. All the emotions at once. Jason knew this and used the affectionate term frequently when they talked.

They hung up their respective phones, and Jason exited the prison. Sitting in his truck, he thought back to the first time he had heard from Corey. Jason had volunteered for an inmate pen pal program through his church. He had written to several names on the list and Corey was one of the few that actually responded. The first few letters they had exchanged were handwritten on lined notebook paper. These were replaced after a few months by the new online system instituted by the penal system. After that, they had corresponded through the app. They were allowed one written communication per week and one short video call each month.

The conversations started out as expected. Tell me about yourself. What did you do to get locked up? Do you have family? Etc etc. Boring but necessary. One day, during a video call, Corey admitted to Jason that he "wouldn't kick him out of bed if he had the chance." This took Jason by surprise, and he floundered to answer. Ending up with a mumbled "thanks" instead of anything more reasonable.

Later that same evening, Jason was trying to sleep, and he could not get Corey out of his head. The muscled tattooed arms, shaved head, crooked smile, lovable personality. Jason felt a stirring in his groin that was new for him. He looked over to make sure his wife was asleep and slowly stroked his hard cock. With thoughts of this tatted convict and his muscled body, it took mere seconds for him to shoot his load onto his quivering stomach. He silently got out of bed that night and quietly washed himself in the hall bathroom so as not to wake his wife. He did not want to explain this to her. He did not even know how to explain it to himself.

Future conversations, both written and by video, contained strong overtones of sexual innuendos. This was a new thing for Jason and he found he enjoyed these interactions with Corey. He found himself thinking of Corey daily, barely able to wait each week to get a digital letter from him. Their video calls eventually turned to talk of sexual preferences. Jason was shy about admitting what was on his mind, and Corey was very vocal and direct. Often telling Jason that he wanted to bend him over the back of a chair and fuck him 'til he passed out. Jason did not fully understand the pleasure Corey got from telling him this, but his dick got rock hard every time Corey talked to him like that.

As time passed, the conversation also turned to fantasies of cuddling, kissing, and other tender moments that might be shared in the future. Jason played along the thoughts of what might happen, frequently occupying his thoughts. But truthfully, he never really thought it would happen. Afterall, Corey was in prison for murder, grand theft auto, and a string of other crimes. Would they really let him out?

But now the time had come where that seemed like a real possibility. Corey's last letter said that he had something big to tell Jason. As Jason initiated the video call, Corey's smiling face appeared, tears running down his face.

"Hey, hey, buddy, what's wrong?" Jason asked, the concern evident in his voice.

"Nothing's wrong, Jason, I'm so happy! My parole was granted!" Corey wiped at his face as he continued to sob. "We can finally be together."

"That's great!" Jason exclaimed. His mind was a blur. What was happening? Was this real? "When do you get out?"

"Three weeks," Corey said. "We won't be able to talk again until then, so I'm going to send the details in a letter on the app. Please, Jason, don't let me down with this."

"Okay, buddy, I'm happy for you. Send me the details." Jason ended the call and sat in silence. What the fuck was he going to do now? Corey was going to get out, and he expected them to get together. Jason had never been with another man. He had never even thought of having sex with another man until he met Corey. Now, it was all he could think about. He would wait for Corey's letter and see what he had in mind.

The letter came a few days later: the date of release, details of when and where to pick him up, what to bring (clothes, a list of very specific snacks, and, of course, lube). Evidently, Corey owned a cabin about an hour drive from the prison. He expected Jason to pick him up, they would drive to the cabin, and spend the following week "getting to know one another." Could he do this? He wasn't sure. He would need to take time off work. And, more importantly, find a really good excuse to tell his wife. Yep, he was going to do it. He made all sorts of excuses in his mind, but he knew, in the end, he would do it.

The day finally arrived. Jason waited in the parking lot of the prison, nervous and excited. He had taken the week off work, told his wife he had a work conference that was last minute (can't believe she bought that one), and had gathered all the requested supplies. The lube was the worst thing to buy. He had no idea what to get and ended up getting a variety of things from the drugstore, including a large pump bottle of lotion. Maybe they could give each other massages? That would be nice.

As Corey exited the prison gate, he spotted Jason stepping out of his truck, waving. Corey trotted over, dropped the small duffle he was carrying, and wrapped his arms around Jason in a tight embrace.

Lifting him off the ground, Corey spun him in circles, tears streaming down his face.

"I can't believe I'm out!" Corey yelled. "Let's go!"

Jason didn't respond. A little stunned, he got in the truck, started the navigation to the address Corey had given him in the letter, and got on the road. They sat in silence for the first 10 minutes.

"Aren't you happy to see me?" Corey asked, hurt apparent in his voice.

"I'm so happy to see you, Corey. I'm also nervous. You know this is all new to me? I just need for you to be patient with me. Please." Jason confessed.

"It's all good, my friend. I got you. It's just you and me." Corey reached his hand over to the back of Jason's neck and gently rubbed it. "We have all week to make this happen. But it's been a long time for me, except prison sex, of course, which isn't the same, so you might have to help me get off when we get there. You okay with that until we figure things out?"

"Yes, of course. Just… just be patient, okay?" Jason hoped he wasn't going to be the reason Corey went back to prison.

"Yep, we will get there. Don't worry."

They soon got the cabin, and Corey got out the truck and ran over to a tree nearby, digging around in the dirt around the roots. Suddenly, he whooped and held up a rusty metal box about the size of a cigar box. "Keys and cash!" he yelled to Jason. He opened the box and dangled a set of keys, one of which he used to open the cabin door.

The cabin was simple. One room with a large fireplace in the center. A large couch and small kitchenette occupied one side, a king-size bed, and wardrobe the other. A door off to the side led to a large bathroom with a big walk-in shower.

"This is nice," Jason remarked.

"Thanks. A friend of mine has been taking care of it for me," Corey said, moving into the cabin and closing the door. He dropped his duffle and grabbed Jason gently at the waist, pulling him towards him. This caused Jason to drop the bags of snacks and other stuff that he was holding. Corey gently placed his lips on Jason's. Easing into something he had not done for years. Jason reciprocated, increasing the pressure on Corey's lips. Their tongues found each other, and the kiss quickly became passionate. Jason's hand found Corey's muscular chest, the light covering of hair felt nice under his fingers. Corey reached down and rubbed Jason's hard cock through his jeans. Corey's other hand unbuttoned his own pants and grabbed his rock-hard cock. Just a few strokes brought him to climax, his lips never leaving Jason's. He shot his load all over Jason's jeans. Corey convulsed, sighed, and then his entire body relaxed.

"I really needed that," he whispered in Jason's ear. "Now we can chill for a bit and get to know each other."

"We'll have to wash my jeans," Jason said.

"By the end of this week, we'll have to wash everything." Corey laughed.

Corey rummaged through the snacks Jason had brought, grabbed a bag of sour cream and onion chips, and settled on the couch. Jason sat at the opposite end and watched him devour the potato chips.

"These are my favorite!" Corey said. "Can't get these inside, for some reason."

"I'm glad you like them," Jason responded. "Hey, Corey. Can we talk for a bit? I'm really nervous about this."

"Of course, my friend. What do you want to talk about?"

"Just expectations for this week. I'm super nervous."

"Let's start out with just being with each other. I think things will go naturally from there. Sound good?" Corey was being very casual about it.

"Yes," Jason agreed.

"Cool. I'm going to take a piss, and then we can get on the bed and talk. I'll meet you there. Get undressed and get under the covers." Corey's tone was firm yet comforting. Corey walked to the bathroom, dropping his pants and underwear along the way. He didn't bother to close the door. "This is going to be a big adjustment," Jason thought.

When Corey finished urinating, he walked towards the bed, pulling his t-shirt over his head on the way. Jason had done as he had been told, waiting nervously, naked, under the covers. He marveled at Corey's body. Lean and muscular, covered in tattoos, Corey was not tall, maybe 5'9" at the most. but his body was perfectly proportioned. Except his dick, which was long and not too thick. The perfectly shaped cock with its big head swung gently against Corey's thighs as he walked towards the bed. Corey got under the covers and released a long sigh.

"Do you know how long it's been since I've been in a real bed?" he asked as he turned to face Jason. "Over twenty years, Jason. So much has changed in the world. I'm nervous about fitting in. I have some money stashed away, so I can take my time looking for a job, and I can live here. So, I think I'm good. But right now, this week, I just want to be with you." Corey started to cry softly. The weight of being released from twenty years of incarceration finally hitting him. Jason moved closer to Corey, pulling him in close.

"Turn over, let me hold you," Jason said. Corey rolled over, and Jason spooned him, holding him tightly in his arms until the sobs subsided. Finally, Corey turned back towards Jason and kissed him gently. Their hands started exploring each other's bodies. Jason was about two inches shorter than Corey. Fit and lean from years of triathlons. He had some body hair but not as much as Corey. Jason's dark hair and green eyes added to a natural attractiveness that contrasted sharply with Corey's edgy look.

Corey's touch was firm and clumsy. It had been a long time since he had experienced this level of intimacy. Eventually, his touch smoothed as his memory reactivated his hands. He ran one hand down Jason's back and firmly squeezed Jason's firm, round butt cheeks, pausing slightly before firmly running a single finger through the crack for a single stroke across Jason's tight hole. Jason tensed at the touch and soon relaxed as Corey's hand made its way to the front, where he grabbed Jason's erection and started to stroke quickly. Jason was not as well-endowed as Corey, perfectly shaped at 5 inches. Jason came almost immediately.

"Whoa, that was almost as quick as me!" Corey chuckled.

"Sorry," Jason muttered.

"It's all good. We both need practice. Put your hand on mine."

Jason wrapped his hand around Corey's throbbing cock. He started pulling like Corey had done with him. Corey moaned loudly. "Fuuuuuuck," he said breathlessly, and his load shot out into Jason's hand. Jason instinctively leaned over and kissed Corey. Corey responded, and they kissed gently for a few minutes until Corey fell asleep. Jason turned on his back, one hand resting softly on Corey's belly, sticky with drying cum. His mind was a whirlwind of confusion, pleasure, relief, and contentment. Soon, Jason drifted off to join Corey in his blissful sleep.

Jason woke to the crinkling sound of a potato chip bag being opened. He blinked sleepily as Corey, completely naked, strutted back to the bed with the bag in hand, shoving handfuls of chips into his mouth as he walked.

"You are the most beautiful thing I've ever seen," Corey mumbled through a mouthful of chips.

"My view's not bad either," Jason said. "Your body is amazing!"

Corey settled on the edge of the bed, offering Jason the bag. Jason grabbed a few chips and ate them calmly. He didn't usually eat in bed. So many new things today. "How was that?" Corey asked.

"Intense," Jason replied. "And I want more," he confessed.

"Easy partner," Corey said in a mock cowboy voice," You'll get plenty of chances to ride this horse." The comment made Jason laugh.

Over the rest of the day, they talked, laughed, kissed, cuddled, generally getting to know each other. They drove to the small town nearby to have dinner. At Corey's request, they ate a sit-down-and-order-at-the-table dinner. The meal was pleasant, and Jason listened attentively to Corey's contract stream of questions about the world that he had missed for the past twenty years.

Once they got back to the cabin, Corey asked Jason if he was ready to take things to the next level. Jason was ready. Corey moved Jason over to the bed and started to undress him. Jason tried to reciprocate, but Corey quickly told him to stop.

"I want to enjoy this. Just let me enjoy you," Corey whispered in Jason's ear as he kissed softly on his neck.

Jason stood naked and uncomfortable as Corey kissed and rubbed every inch of his body. Eventually, Corey told Jason to lie back on the bed. Jason did as he was told. Corey then started to undress himself as Jason watched. He did it slowly, allowing Jason time to watch and enjoy. Once they were both naked, Corey grabbed a bottle of lube and placed it neatly on the bed beside them. He knelt between Jason's spread thighs, grabbed the lube, and squirted some into his hand. His slick fingers pressed gently against Jason's sphincter, feeling it quiver with each stroke. Jason allowed himself to relax into the sensation. It felt amazing and strange. The new sensation made his dick so hard he thought it would explode.

"Okay, lover, I'm going to put the head of my cock against your hole. When it's there, I want you to squeeze with your hole. Squeeze as tight as you can. Okay?"

"Okay, buddy, please go slow." Jason was nervous and excited.

Jason did as he was told. He squeezed his sphincter as much as he could against the intruding head of Corey's hard dick. When he could hold it no more, he released. The moment he released, Corey pushed gently in, inserting his entire big cock into Jason's waiting hole. Jason gasped at the sensation. There was a strange combination of pain and pleasure. Corey remained very still, allowing Jason's body to adjust.

"You okay?" Corey asked.

"I'm good. Just need to breathe," Jason responded.

Corey leaned in and kissed Jason, maintaining the position of his cock. As Jason relaxed, Corey started sliding his hard cock in and out slowly. Never completely exiting and always pushing in as far as it would go. After only a few strokes, his motions quickened. He grabbed Jason's cock and started stroking. There was residual lube on his hand that heightened the sensation for Jason.

"I'm going to cum!" Jason gasped as he emptied into Corey's hand and his belly. At the same moment, Corey shoved his dick in hard and emptied his load into Jason with a loud yell. His entire body convulsed with the intensity of the orgasm. He collapsed down on top of Jason. Jason's arms reached around and pulled Corey tightly to him as Corey's softening dick slid out. They maintained that tight hug for several minutes before Corey rolled off and positioned himself beside Jason. They held hands in silence as they both drifted off to sleep.

About half an hour later, Jason woke to Corey snoring softly beside him, both of them still uncovered from the previous activity. Jason got out of bed and made his way to the shower. He turned on the water and allowed it to become hot before stepping in and getting himself wet.

He had only been in the shower a few minutes when Corey stepped in. "Showering without me?" Corey laughed.

"I didn't want to wake you. You look like an angel when you sleep."

"Well, I'm no angel, as you know." Corey pulled Jason to him and kissed him deeply under the stream of the shower. Jason grabbed a bottle of body wash, and they lathered each other up before rinsing off.

"No soap to drop, what a shame." Corey smiled as water ran over his shaved head and down his face.

"Funny," Jason smirked, laughing with him.

Corey leaned in close to Jason, "I want you to fuck me."

"Now?" Jason asked.

"Yes, now. You got a problem with that?" Corey seemed forceful.

"No, no, I just don't know what I'm doing," Jason admitted.

"I'll guide you, just do what I say." They were both hard from the short conversation. Corey slid his soapy hand up his butt crack, getting it very wet and slippery, then turned around to face away from Jason.

"Just put it against my hole, I'll ease onto it," Corey said. Jason pressed against Corey's back, and with a small movement of Corey's hips, his cock slid effortlessly into Corey. The sensation was intense as Corey's tight hole squeezed Jason's erect dick. Corey started grinding against Jason, doing all the work. "Grab my cock," Corey commanded. Jason did, and that was all it took. His orgasm was strong as he dropped his load into Corey's ass. Jason's hand continued to move around Corey's erection involuntarily. Corey's release was not far behind Jason's. Pulling out, Jason rinsed himself as Corey did the same under the single shower head.

After drying off, Jason wrapped a towel around himself as Corey proudly strutted around completely naked. They walked to the kitchen,

Corey grabbing a glass from the counter and filling it with water from the tap, before tugging at the towel wrapped around Jason.

"I want you naked," he said.

"I'm not used to walking naked," Jason said with some force.

"Yeh, well, GET used to it," Corey responded as he pulled the towel completely off and threw it on the floor. Jason was not sure what to do, so he just went with it. Was it really that bad to be naked in front of this man, especially considering what had happened over the past few hours. So he did. He remained unclothed. He was surprised at how freeing it felt.

He and Corey sat on the sofa. Naked. Corey's legs spread wide, showing that he was completely comfortable in this environment. Over the next few days, they got to know each other. And practiced their intimacy. A lot. Jason quickly became a pro at fucking, both taking and receiving. The sensation became more intense with each session. And true to his word, Corey bent him over the couch and fucked him 'til he almost passed out. And Jason loved it.

What was next? Neither of them knew. But they did know they would figure it out. Corey was free, and Jason had found a new hobby. Life is good after parole.

6: Alien Abduction

Levi felt the weight of the room before he even opened his eyes—an odd, stifling pressure as if the very air pressed down on his chest. Something was wrong. The slow, labored sound of breathing at his side jolted him fully awake. Blinking in the dim light, he turned his head to the side and saw Blaine lying on a strange, rigid surface that looked more grown than built. Alarm coursed through Levi as he checked Blaine's face, searching for any sign of injury.

"Blaine," he said, low and urgent, turning on his side and giving his friend's shoulder a gentle shake. "Blaine!"

With a ragged breath, Blaine's eyelids fluttered open. He bolted upright, hand slapping his hip for a firearm that wasn't there. Confusion flickered across his face as he glanced from his own hairy chest to Levi's, which was mostly bare with a dusting of light brown hair. His gaze traveled down Levi's body, and noticed that he was completely naked. Levi's muscular body nicely framed an ample cock that rested lazily against one thigh. He felt a strange stir in his pelvis as his eyes moved back up to Levi's handsome face and tousled brown hair. Blaine's eyebrows raised in silent questions: Where were their clothes? Their gear? And most importantly… where were they?

Levi could only shrug, equally puzzled. Blaine signaled with two fingers: first to Levi, then toward the door. Without a word, they slipped off the hard organic platform they'd been sprawled on. As soon as their bare feet touched the floor, a scraping noise sounded from beyond the doorway. Heart pounding, Levi pressed himself against one side of the frame, Blaine mirroring him on the other. Their nakedness momentarily forgotten, they held their breath, waiting for whoever—or whatever—might enter.

The scraping continued, then faded, moving on without stopping. In the tense silence, Levi and Blaine exchanged grim looks. They needed answers—and a way to defend themselves. A quick scan of the chamber showed a uniquely alien environment, sinewy walls, and the single organic surface they'd woken up on. Nothing close to a weapon.

Tension mounted as Levi's mind whirled: Who brought them here? Where was their equipment? Anger simmered in his chest, but he forced it down, catching Blaine's gaze, he was briefly distracted by the sight of Levi standing naked beside him, his hazel eyes accentuated by the scruff of beard and shaved head. He quickly re-gained focus and looked Blaine directly in the eyes. In that moment, they silently reaffirmed their resolve: they would get out of this—together.

They just had to figure out how.

Levi broke the quiet. "Do you remember anything? Because I don't. I was at home—alone, with no witnesses, doing nothing illegal—just burying a perfectly normal, non-dangerous object in my backyard. Then everything went sideways, and now we're clearly in some alien-created confinement area. Gotta admire the all-natural vibe… even if it comes with kidnapping. Seriously, though—an alien abduction? Could these guys get any more cliché?"

Levi's gaze darted to the door one last time, verifying they were alone. Then he grasped Blaine's arm and pulled him closer, his hand trailing over Blaine's muscled chest. His fingers threaded through the thick chest hair, lingering for just a second before sliding up to cup the back of Blaine's neck. Blaine tensed and started to pull away before melting back towards Levi.

"While we're here alone…" Levi murmured, voice hushed. He leaned in, pressing a hard kiss against the side of Blaine's neck, the warmth of his breath sending a shiver over Blaine's skin. Levi's mouth traveled upward, his lips seeking Blaine's in a bold, hungry kiss that made them both forget—if only for a moment—where they were. Blaine reciprocated Levi's advances, his tongue finding Levi's and pressing hard into him as only two men could do.

A low sound of appreciation escaped Blaine's throat. He moved closer, one hand slipping around Levi's waist, the other lifting to cradle Levi's jaw. Blaine pulled Levi into him, their now erect cocks brushing against each other playfully. Blaine's dick was massive. At least eight inches; thick with a well-defined head. This massive member now rested tightly between their stomachs while Levi's shorter cock found its way under Blaine's balls and applied gentle pressure upwards into Blaine's taint.

Their bare chests brushed together, the sensation of skin on skin a fleeting reminder of the danger they were in—and, strangely, the comfort they found in each other's presence — their shared masculinity providing a strong sense of protection.

Blaine nuzzled his face into the nape of Levi's neck and released a forceful sigh of pleasure. For a heartbeat, they allowed themselves this rare pause: the tension, the curiosity, the fear slipping into the background. Then, the reality of their confinement surged back. With a lingering touch, Blaine pulled away, resting his forehead against Levi's bare chest.

"We'll get out of here," Blaine breathed, voice low and resolute. "But for now…"

Levi smirked, kissing the top of Blaine's shaved head. "For now, we make the most of what we've got."

Blaine slid his hand down Levi's chest and fingered the top ridge of his pubic hair, noting that Levi was eagerly responding to his touch. "Danger with you makes me so eager for you," breathed Blaine. "I'm so into you right now!"

"Not as much as I'm into you!" Levi responded, pushing Blaine back onto the alien bed platform.

Levi forcefully spread Blaine's legs and greedily buried his face in Blaine's crotch, taking all of his massive cock into his mouth in one wet gulp. Blaine moaned loudly, his rock-hard cock throbbing as Levi's lips slid up and down over the head. Just as he thought he would not last any longer, Levi re-positioned his face to match Blaine's. The kissing that ensued was passionate and urgent. Their hands exploring every part of each other's bodies that could be reached in their current position.

"Okay, my turn," Blaine whispered in Levi's ear. With the agility of the special forces soldier that he was, he strongly flipped Levi over onto his back and continued kissing him, moving from his lips to his ear lobes finally to Levi's neck.

Blaine stopped the kisses for a moment and let his full weight settle on Levi's body. He pulled his face up and moved his hands to cradle each side of Levi's face. "Levi…..I didn't know until just now how much I've wanted this."

"Me too, my friend. I realize now that I've always wanted you," Levi whispered back.

With that, Blaine continued to show Levi just how "into him" he was. His lips moved to Levi's right nipple, which he sucked and flicked with his tongue. This produced deep moans from Levi which told Blaine he was making the right moves. As he abandoned the nipple, Blaine allowed his tongue to trace the muscles of Levi's abdomen, making his way slowly down towards the area where he really wanted to be.

After playfully enjoying Levi's lightly hairy belly, Blaine moved his mouth to Levi's beautiful dick, which had been teasing his chest and neck up to now. Levi's cock was perfect. Six inches, a nicely defined head, and a slight curve upwards. It was perfect for Blaine to fit entirely in his mouth so that his tongue could lick the tight balls below.

Blaine sucked lightly at the head of Levi's cock. He flicked his tongue on the underside of the glans, which seemed to make Levi crazy with ecstasy. He would have to remember this area for future play if they ever escaped this place. Blaine continued pleasuring Levi by licking lightly at his balls and tracing the entire path of his genitals up to the head and back down again. He settled finally with a gentle motion of moving Levi's rock-hard cock between his lips while he flicked at the underside with the tip of his tongue.

Levi could hold out no longer. With a hard thrust, he grabbed Blaine's head with both hands as he forced his pulsing dick into Blaine's throat and released his load. Blaine swallowed without hesitation. Levi allowed his arms to collapse on either side of his body. Blaine moved himself to his side, gently stroking Levi's chest with his fingers. Blaine's still-hard dick rested firmly on Levi's thigh.

"Give me a minute to recover, and I'll take care of you." Levi said breathlessly.

"Take your time, my friend. I really enjoyed that, and judging from your reaction, you did too!?" Blaine grinned at Levi.

That smile. Levi could not resist it. He pushed Blaine back and immediately took his entire eight inches into his mouth. Mimicking

Blaine's previous routine, it took a very short time to bring Blaine to climax. Reciprocating the favor, Levi swallowed it all and continued to lick and suck until Blaine had to ask him to stop. "Come cuddle with me," Blaine instructed.

Levi nestled his head on Baine's furry chest, content, his breath even and peaceful. Blaine stroked Levi's hair gently, occasionally bending his head to kiss the top of Levi's head. Together, they fell asleep in this position. Forgetting where they were and what dangers might be coming. Their only thoughts were of this newfound connection and what that might mean for their friendship.

In the control room of the alien ship, the two aliens looked at the screen that showed the containment room where Levi and Blaine were being held.

"It happened just as you predicted," one of them said.

"Yes, I knew it would. Let's provide some nourishment for them while they sleep and a few more comfort items. We will keep them isolated for a few days to see if they repeat this behavior."

"And what if they do?" The first alien queried.

"Then we will know that this bond might be the strongest. We will need to encourage the behavior among friends who exhibit this same attraction. It might be crucial in future battles."

7: Target Acquired

James stepped out of the locker room shower and grabbed his towel from the hook on the wall. One of the advantages of being an Air Force Colonel was having a private locker room dedicated to senior officers. The gym on the Air Force base in Shreveport, LA, was large, and the main locker room was usually crowded. Having access to the smaller locker room was convenient, to say the least. Although small, the senior officer locker room was well-equipped with a small bank of lockers, a single stall and urinal, a vanity with two sinks, and a four-person gang shower. There was a small antiquated dry sauna built into one wall, but James had never known it to work, evidenced by a dog-eared sign on the door. He was usually the only one in the locker room, and he enjoyed walking around naked after a shower, allowing his hairy, muscular frame to air-dry. His light brown hair was cropped short and belied his actual age. Keeping fit and eating well turned his forty-nine years into an appearance of mid-thirties.

As James stood naked in front of this locker, the electronic lock on the door clicked, and the door opened with a slight creak. That was odd, he thought. There was never anyone in this locker room at 0600. James was curious what other senior officer would be working out this early in the morning. He grabbed his towel from its location hanging on the open locker door and wrapped it around his waist. The tuck which held it in place accentuated the six-pack that was clearly visible beneath the fur on his belly.

The gentleman that walked around the corner was younger than James. Maybe early thirties, average height, with sandy blond hair. The man stopped and looked at James, obviously surprised to see someone else in here. James looked up from the bench where he was arranging his uniform.

"Good morning." James said firmly. "I'm usually the only one in here. I'm Colonel James McGuinn."

"Uhh, Good morning, Sir. Second Lieutenant Matt Miller. 2nd Maintenance Group," the man responded.

"Good to meet you." James extended his right hand for a shake, mindful to hold the towel in place with his left. "You know this is the senior officer's locker room, right?"

"Yes, sir. Apologies. I'll go to the main one. There's never anyone in here, so I take my chances." Matt gave a nervous laugh as he shouldered his gym bag and started to turn around.

"Nah, it's all good. Stay. It's nice to have some company," James said with a chuckle.

"Thank you, Colonel McGuinn. I won't get in your way, I promise." Matt smiled and moved to a locker at the opposite end of the single row of lockers from where James was standing.

"First, in here, call me Jamie. That's what my friends call me. Save the Colonel for outside the gym," James offered.

"Yes, Sir. I mean… thanks, Jamie." Matt stumbled over his words.

James silently turned back to his uniform as Matt started undressing in front of his locker. James couldn't help but sneak covert peeks as Matt undressed. He was very fit. Lean and muscular, with very little body hair. The muscles of his back rippled as he donned his t-shirt. James couldn't help but stare as Matt removed his pants and underwear, revealing a long cock and low-hanging balls that swung gently between his legs. The tuft of blond pubic hair perfectly accented his beautiful endowment. James himself had never been shy about the size of his penis. It was shorter than most but exceptionally thick, with a large mushroom head that swelled gloriously when erect. James could feel the engorgement starting, so he quickly dried off and pulled on his underwear, turning slightly towards Matt to see if he would look.

James was pleased to see that Matt was trying to conceal his gaze. James looked at him and winked, turning his back to Matt to finish getting dressed. He could feel Matt's gaze focused on his firm, furry ass. By the time he had loaded his gym bag, Matt was fully changed and ready for his workout. James gathered his things and headed towards the door.

"I'm here most mornings at 0530, by the way," James mentioned as he exited the room and allowed the door to close behind him.

The following morning, James arrived at the gym at his usual 0530. He expected the locker room to be empty, relatively sure that Matt would not have taken the hint. As he opened the door and stepped around the corner, he encountered Matt standing at the locker directly next to the one that James always used. Matt was slowly unpacking his gym bag. He looked up and smiled at James. Matt's smile was bright, engaging, and somewhat disarming for James.

"I was hoping you would be here," James said. "Do you want to workout together?"

"Yes, please. I was kinda hoping that was what would happen," Matt responded.

"Cool. Let's get changed and get to it." James was curious how this would end.

The two men quickly changed into their workout clothes, sneaking glances at the other when they thought the other wasn't looking. They exited the locker room and talked about what the workout would look like. As they made their way to the room with free weights, James cold not help but notice how sexy Josh looked in his tight 3-inch shorts and snug t-shirt. His arms and thighs pushed forcefully against the fabric as he moved. Throughout the workout, James couldn't help but stare at Matt's body as his muscles flexed under the strain of the weights. Occasionally, he would catch Matt staring at him in the same way. Fantasies flooded his mind about where this might lead, making it difficult for him to focus on the workout.

"Shower, then breakfast?" Matt had finished his last set, and the adrenaline seemed to have removed inhibitions and shyness.

"Sounds like a fantastic plan," James replied, shooting Matt a smile. James had failed to notice the depth of blue of Matt's eyes. The morning light filtering through the gym's skylights caused the hue to shift like liquid. James' eyes were deep brown. A physical trait that he had resented as a teen but had grown to enjoy as an adult. The combination of muscles, body hair, and brown eyes had attracted many lovers over the years.

Back in the locker room, James was the first to undress, allowing Matt to get a good look at him as he walked slowly to the showers.

"Don't be all day," James said, entered the four-head gang shower.

Matt quickly followed, his ample dick slapping against his inner thigh as he walked quickly to join James in shower room. James had already turned on the water to his showerhead, letting the hot water wash over his body. Matt turned on the water to the showerhead next to James and started to later his body with gel from the dispenser attached to the wall. James could see that Matt's cock was partially erect. This caused James' dick to get immediately rock-hard, protruding outward from his crotch with a very slight upward curve. One glance at James' erection and Matt's cock joined the party. Matt's dick had a slight downward hang when hard, aligning with the exceptional length.

James turned to directly face Matt, reached out and grabbed his soapy dick, and pulled him forcefully towards him. Their lips met, mouths opened, and tongues battled with a testosterone-fueled passion that had been building since the day before. James's hand gently stroked Matt's hard cock, the wet shower gel providing lubrication as the ridges on the underside of his hand repeatedly rubbed across all sides of the head. Matt returned the favor with Jame's engorged dick.

"Fuck, your cock is so damn thick!" Matt whispered in James's ear. Their strokes quickened, their lips hovering millimeters apart but not touching, as their breathing quickened. James was the first to shoot his load, followed seconds later by Matt. The two men stood facing each other, eyes maintaining contact as they silently rinsed off. They walked out of the shower, grabbed their towels, and each dried their own bodies as they walked back to the lockers. Their silence protrinued as they dressed.

"Same time tomorrow?" James asked as he left the locker room, not waiting for a response. Walking to his truck, he knew that Matt was still standing in the locker room. Wondering what the fuck had just happened. If Matt showed up tomorrow, James had a different plan in mind.

James arrived early to the gym the next day and had already changed into running shorts by the time Matt arrived. James had purposefully donned only the shorts. No shirt, no shoes. Matt placed his clothes neatly in the locker and pulled on a pair of shorts as James watched. Matt gave him a show, moving slowly and turning to give James a good view of all sides, leaving his shirt off to match James. This had the effect Matt wanted, as evidenced in the tented nature of James' shorts.

"What's the workout plan for the day? Assuming we're going for a run?" Matt queried.

"How about some cardio?" James answered as he took Matt's hand and led him to the defunct sauna.

Once inside, James pulled Matt close to him and kissed him hard on the mouth, his tongue probing to find Matt's. Matt reciprocated, pressing his entire body into James'. Matt's hands explored James' furry chest with his fingers, relishing in the softness of the hair with the firm muscle underneath.

"I want you inside me. You okay with that?" James said firmly as he looked Matt directly in the eyes.

"Oh, yes. I'm going to fuck you hard enough to get my cardio in for the day," Matt responded, matching James' gaze.

James pulled a single-use pack of lube from the waistband of his shorts and tore the tab off with his teeth. Squeezing the lube into his hand, he rubbed a liberal amount onto Matt's throbbing cock, then reached back and deposited the remaining between his hot, hairy crack. He then turned to face the sauna wall, reached back to grab Matt's long dick, and positioned the head against his waiting hole. Without hesitation, Matt reached up with his left hand and grabbed James' shoulder, his right hand grabbing the base of his cock as he attempted to slowly enter James. As soon as James felt Matt's head enter, he pushed back hard, taking all eight inches of Matt's engorged member. James groaned in pleasure as Matt's cock filled every inch of his hairy hole.

"Whoa," Matt exclaimed. "That was intense. You really wanted it!"

"It feels so good. I've been wanting this since I first saw that gorgeous dick of yours."

Matt started to slowly slide his cock in and out, allowing the head to barely escape James' quivering hole before shoving it back in James' assisted by rocking his hips in rhythm to Matt's motion, getting as deep as possible with each grind. When Matt's strokes started getting quicker, James pushed back hard, forcing Matt to sit on the seat in the Sauna. Matt's hands grabbed James' hips as James leaned back on Matt's chest, grabbing his own thick cock. He started stroking himself, moving his fingers over the large head as he ground down on Matt's erection to get it as deep inside him as it could possibly go.

"Don't stop," James commanded. "I'm going to shoot my load." Matt kept pumping as James unloaded his massive load on to the wall of the sauna. Before James had finished cumming, Matt's increased hip thrusts indicated that he was close.

"I'm going to cum!" Matt said breathlessly.

"Don't pull out! Cum inside me!" James pushed further onto Matt, preventing him from pulling out. With one final thrust, Matt came hard, unloading his jizz into James' hungry hole. James leaned back farther and grabbed Matt's hair with his hand, pulling Matt's lips to his own. They kissed deeply as Matt's body shuddered from the orgasm.

Matt collapsed back on the wooden bench. James deftly extricated himself from Matt's crotch and settled beside him on the bench. At that moment, they heard the sound of the electronic lock of the door to the locker room.

"Be quiet!" James whispered.

They sat in silence for at least five minutes while watching through the small window as an attendant checked the supplies. Thankfully, the window was worn, and the sauna dark. While they waited in the tense darkness, Matt's hand found James' thigh and started to rub it lightly, moving very slowly towards his crotch. The thought of being naked in the sauna and possibly being caught revived James' erection. He was surprised that he could recover to so quickly after such an intense orgasm. Matt's hand wrapped around James' hard cock and started to stroke lightly and playfully. They heard the door close as the attendant left, and James immediately reached over to find that Matt's dick had recovered as well and was harder than ever.

"My turn." Matt whispered, giving James a quick but forceful kiss.

James sat up on the bench to protest, but Matt was quicker. He straddled James, facing him, and lowered himself onto James' groin. He ground against James' thick cock, letting it playfully tease his hole. Matt spat in his hand, reached back, and made his hole as wet as possible. Positioning James' cock in just the right spot, he applied slow and deliberate pressure. The massive head entered Matt, and he gave a slight gasp as it filled his tight hole. James' pulled Matt to him and started kissing him passionately, moving his hips in circles to assist the entry. When he was fully inside, it only took a few strokes for him to unload. Matt's hole was super tight, and the way he touched James brought the climax quickly.

Matt allowed James to stay inside him as he softened, stroking his own dick methodically, and he continued to kiss James. It did not take long for him to cum. His jizz covered both their abdomen, making a sticky mess that glued them together. Their mouths never lost contact. Exhausted, Matt collapsed on top of James as James' arms wrapped around Matt and pulled him close.

"How was that for cardio?" James asked.

"Better than a run, that's for sure," Matt replied.

"Let's wash up, and I'll buy you breakfast. I know a place that has fantastic burritos."

"Great! I've definitely worked up an appetite."

They checked to make sure the coast was clear before exiting the sauna, walked the five feet to the showers, and washed themselves.

James couldn't help himself as he teased Matt by touching his dick and ass while looking the other way and pretending it was an accident. They laughed and joked about their new plan for getting cardio in. They ate burritos in James' truck and generally got to know one another. They talked about the necessity of keeping this private. James wasn't sure where this would go, but he did know one thing – he had a new friend – with benefits.

8: Passion in Provence

The village of Saint-Clément d'Orque had a charm that seemed to defy time. Tucked into the rolling hills of Provence, its cobblestone streets, faded pastel shutters, and lavender-scented breezes felt like a gentle embrace to those who wandered through its quiet paths. For Blake and Marc, it was home—a place where they had chosen to spend their retirement after decades in bustling city life. Blake, an attorney, had retired early at the age of 60. His rugged good looks, dark hair and beard, and muscular, hairy body were at odds with the image that most people associated with those that practiced law. He had made a successful career for himself, focusing on personal injury law. It was never his intention to work past the age of 60. His goal had always been to earn just enough to retire in Europe and enjoy the years he had left.

Marc had taken a very different route from Blake in his career. He started small at the tender age of 18 with one flower shop in the city.

Over the years, he had grown his empire to 5 locations, his intention always being to sell the shops for an early retirement. When he had met Blake in his 50's, he realized that his plan was solid. He and Blake could retire to Europe and make up for the years they had missed. Marc was the perfect complement to Blake. His sandy blonde hair and fit body belied his actual age. Mostly hairless, with just a small dusting of fuzz across his belly and chest, he had immediately fallen in love with the way Blake's body hair felt against his. That was 10 years ago and the intensity of attraction between them had only increased over the years.

The move to Saint-Clément had been a mutual dream. In their second year together, they had driven around France on an impromptu vacation and had discovered the small town completely by accident. They had canceled the remainder of their trip that year and had spent two weeks in a bed and breakfast in the heart of the village. They knew at that moment that this is where they would retire.

Their mornings began at Café du Tilleul, a small, family-run spot nestled in the village square. Each day, they would sit at the same table beneath the shade of an ancient Plane tree, its broad leaves dappling sunlight onto the worn wood of their table. The café was mere steps from the cottage they had purchased two years prior. The small two-bedroom home had all they needed, including a terrace with beautiful views of the village and rooms that were large enough for them to have their own space when needed.

Blake, a meticulous planner, enjoyed reading the local news on his phone, while Marc, by contrast, loved leaning back in his chair, his arms lazily resting on the sides as he observed the life around them—the baker's delivery boy speeding past on his bike, the florist arranging blooms in her window, and the elderly men engaged in heated games of pétanque.

"Croissant?" Blake asked, pushing the basket toward Marc.

Marc grinned. "You ask as if you're expecting me to say no."

They laughed, their voices blending into the morning symphony of clinking cups and soft chatter. After breakfast, they strolled through the village, hand in hand, as was customary in this open, accepting community. The locals had embraced them warmly, often greeting them with a hearty Bonjour, messieurs! The grocer would wave them in to taste the freshest fruits, and the cheese monger would set aside the best rounds of brie, knowing how much Marc adored it. They enjoyed this daily shopping adventure that would lead them to their evening meal.

After a brief visit at the local farmer's market, they made their way along the small river to a natural area where they sometimes rested and had a light snack of bread and cheese. Today, they were still full from croissant, so they simply walked casually along the bubbling water, silent in the comfort of being with one another. They sat on a bench, facing the water, in an area that was secluded from the main thoroughfare. As they sat in silence, Blake reached his hand out to rest lightly on Marc's thigh.

"You mean the world to me, Marc," Blake said softly. "I can't imagine a better life than the one I have with you."

"Ditto, my love," Marc replied, echoing their common banter.

Blake's hand slowly slid up Marc's thigh, feeling evidence of his continuing attraction.

"What are you doing?" Marc teased.

"What?! There's no one around. Let's have a little fun," Blake said naughtily.

Blake started rubbing Marc's growing bulge, eventually moving his hand to Marc's belt buckle, which he loosed with the ease of a professional escort. The button on Marc's khakis followed, along with the zipper. As Blake's fingers found their way into Marc's underwear, Marc moaned quietly at the sensation of Blake's fingertips touching the base of his now throbbing and erect penis. Blake didn't stop. His hand moved further down to fully grasp Marc's rock-hard dick. Marc's penis was short but incredibly thick. Blake could not feel his fingertips touch as he gently squeezed the shaft.

Marc arched his back at the pleasure, his hands pressed firmly on the bench. Blake continued to stroke his cock, whispering in his ear how hard he was going to fuck him when they got back to the cottage.

"Face down. Just like you like it. Hard and slow. In and out. My big cock penetrating your hole. Owning it. Taking it. Making it mine." Blake's words were exactly what Marc wanted to hear. In seconds, he shot his load into Blake's hand.

Blake moved his lips to Marc's, kissing him fiercely.

"That's exactly what you're going to get later tonight," Blake whispered as he allowed Marc to watch while he licked the jizz from his hand. Blake's other hand expertly did up Marc's pants and buckled his belt. Marc never understood how Blake had this talent. He could do with one hand what most people found difficult with two.

They sat in silence for a few minutes, Marc's head resting softly on Blake's shoulder. An air of contentment settled on them, like dew on the flowers of a spring morning. Marc was truly content. He could not have imagined that his life would turn out this way. The perfect partner in the perfect setting. It was everything he needed and everything he could possibly desire.

They started on the walk back to the center of the village, hand in hand. Their favorite walk led them up a winding path to an old stone chapel on the hilltop. From there, they could see the entirety of the village and the vineyards stretching to the horizon. Their cottage was adjacent to the chapel, and they would frequently sit on a weathered bench near the chapel, the distant hum of cicadas occasionally providing a soundtrack to their quiet moments together.

They entered the cottage and paused just inside the door. Blake pulled Marc close and hugged him tightly.

"I never thought retirement could be this peaceful," Blake admitted, his voice tinged with wonder.

"Peaceful, but never dull," Marc teased, nudging him gently.

"True. Life with us is never dull," Blake smiled.

Most evenings were spent in the cozy stone cottage on the edge of the village. The cottage was modest but full of character—its thick walls kept it cool in the summer, and its terracotta roof glowed warmly in the golden hour light.

Marc had taken to cooking, a hobby he had discovered later in life. Dinner was always an event: freshly baked bread, a bottle of local wine, and dishes inspired by the vibrant flavors of Provence. The components of the meal consisted of whatever they could find at the market that day. There was always bread, and there was always cheese. This was a life that Blake found satisfying. Blake would set the table on their terrace, where the scent of rosemary and thyme from their garden mingled with the cool evening air.

As they dined, they shared stories from their pasts—Blake's tales of the craziness of personal injury law and Marc's adventures dealing with bridezillas at weddings where nature had not made the exact color of white in the peonies that the bride had specifically envisioned. They also dreamed of the future, though their dreams were less grand now and more rooted in the simple pleasures of life: planting more lavender in the garden, exploring the nearby coast, or hosting a dinner for their growing circle of village friends.

After dinner, they would linger, watching the stars emerge one by one in the vast, inky sky, slowly finishing the bottle of wine. The quiet intimacy of those moments—the shared glances, the comfortable silences, the warmth of Marc's hand resting on Blake's—was a testament to the life they had built together. And most evenings were accompanied by a level of intimacy envied by most couples. Some nights were spent simply cuddling on the sofa while reading or watching a movie. Others were spent like tonight. An unleashing of passion that would make Eros envious.

It started in the kitchen while cleaning up the dishes from the evening meal. Marc had made a delicious veal shank with roasted root vegetables and fresh bread with local butter. Blake had sopped up the salty gravy with gusto, constantly exclaiming how thankful he was that Marc was such a good cook. Typical of their post-meal ritual, they cleared the table together and settled at the kitchen sink to wash the dishes. Marc would wash while Blake rinsed and placed the dishes on the rack to air dry.

As Blake rinsed the last plate, he leaned his head on Marc's shoulder, gently kissing his neck. His hand reaching into the soapy dishwater and then quickly down the back of Marc's pants. His soapy middle finger expertly finding Marc's warm hole. Blake stroked and probed gently as Marc moaned softly.

"What you do to me, Blake...it's so intense!" Marc whispered in Blakes ear as he turned to face Blake. Blake pressed into Marc's lips, his tongue finding Marc's. Blake's finger continued to prepare Marc's hungry hole for what was to come. As soon as he had started, Blake abruptly pulled away, forcefully turned Marc to face the sink, and pressed his crotch firmly against Marc's round ass. Marc responded by pressing back hard into Blake, feeling the incredible bulge that had developed in Blake's pants.

Blake, with his usual skill, reached around with one hand and quickly released Marc's belt and pants. He hooked his thumbs in the side of the loosened pants, grabbing the underwear as well, and pulled them slowly to the ground. Blake's left hand reached up to the center of Marc's back and forced him to bend over the cooling dishwater.

His other hand loosened his own pants and allowed them to drop casually to the floor, stepping out of them as his bare feet kicked them to the side.

Blake moved both hands to Marc's firm ass cheeks and dropped to his knees. He placed both thumbs on Marc's hole, massaging in slow circles before pulling his cheeks apart and blowing gently on Marc's now quivering hole. Blake's tongue flicked and probed at Marc's anus, performing acrobatic circles and strokes. He varied his attention to occasionally lick and suck at Marc's balls and taint, making sure to allow saliva to fall from his mouth, wetting Marc's ready hole.

Blake stood and placed the head of his hard dick against Marc's pulsing hole. Blake's penis was not as thick as Marc's, but it was much longer, with a well-defined head and a slight curve that sent Marc over the edge when it was inside him.

"You ready for this?" Blake whispered over Marc's shoulder.

"Push it in fast and fuck me hard, Blake. Do it now." Marc wanted Blake's cock so bad. He loved the way it felt in him. He loved the way Blake made love to him. The way Blake knew every pleasure point. Blake grabbed Marc's hips and shoved his erect dick hard into Marc's waiting hole. Marc gasped with a sharp intake of breath as the full nine inches of Blake's cock entered him. Blake pushed in fully and stopped moving, allowing Marc to fully accommodate him.

"You okay?" Blake checked in.

"I'm so good, babe. I want your load in me, now fuck me hard and fast."

Blake pulled his cock back until the head was almost out, then thrust it in again. He repeated this motion, slow out, fast in, knowing it to be Marc's favorite stroke. Blake's motions quickened, and his thrusts became more forceful. He reached around to find Marc's dick so hard and pulsing that it felt like it would soon explode. Blake's fingers massaged the underside of the head of Marc's cock as his strokes became even quicker. Marc shot his load almost immediately after Blake grabbed his cock. The feel of Marc's jizz on his hand caused Blake to cum. His final thrust deposited a large load in Marc's ass. Blake's jizz-covered hand reached up to Marc's mouth, where he inserted his wet fingers and pulled back hard on Marc's head as his orgasm subsided.

Blake collapsed on top of Marc, both of them breathing heavily.

"Every time is better than the last," Blake said breathlessly.

"I know, my love. You always know just what to do to make it great every time," Marc responded.

"I love you, Marcus," Blake whispered, gently kissing Marc's ear.

"I love you, too, Blake. So much."

As they made their way to the shower, Blake teased Marc by slapping his bare ass. Marc turned and looked over his shoulder at Blake as he walked to the bathroom. "Keep doing that, and you're going to have to take care of me again soon," Marc teased back.

"I'm up for it if you are," Blake winked at Marc.

They showered together, washing each other slowly and methodically. Lightly kissing each other. Marc would occasionally lean his head on Blake's chest and hold him tightly under the hot water from the shower, the shared sense of contentment evident between them.

After the shower, they settled in by a small fire in the stone fireplace. Marc sat at one end of the sofa with a book while Blake reclined at the other end, his feet in Marc's lap. Blake turned on the television and watched an episode of a reality show while the sun set and the evening moved on.

"Ready for bed?" Marc asked, closing his book and placing it on the side table.

"Yes, let's do it," Blake responded as he stretched his arms above him and yawned.

They moved to the bathroom, each completing their nightly routine, taking their meds, brushing their teeth, applying night-time face cream. Marc made it to bed first, cozily settling his naked body under the covers. Blake walked lazily from the bathroom, his long dick gently slapping his thighs as he walked. Marc always tried to be the first in bed. He loved watching Blake walk naked from the bathroom. He pulled back the covers and settled in next to Marc, turning to face him and pulling him close. Marc's hand caressed Blake's furry chest, moving down to his stomach, then his crotch, where he found evidence of Blake's intent. Marc moved his groin closer to Blake, signaling his acceptance by pressing his also hard cock against Blake's thigh.

Marc moved his lips to Blake's and kissed him gently, progressing to an unbridled passion as Blake returned the kiss. Their tongues danced around each other as their hands slowly stroked each other's cocks. Marc rolled on top of Blake, extending his body to align with Blake's, their erections firmly pressed together. Blake's hips thrust up and down, pulling Marc slightly towards him so that his dick was free to rub against Marc's crack.

Marc reached over to the nightstand and grabbed the bottle of lube, squirting a generous amount into his hand before depositing it on his hole. He quickly spread the remaining amount on Blake's erect penis, focusing on gently lubricating the engorged head. Blake moaned. Marc knew his sensitive areas. Marc's hand returned to his own hole, his fingers massaging it as his back arched, getting it ready for Blake.

Blake grabbed Marc's hand and pulled it away from his self-stimulation. He guided is rock-hard cock to meet Marc's slick hole. With intentional paced rhythm, Blake pushed the head of his cock against the outside of Marc's anus. He liked teasing Marc like this. Marc moaned, trying to push himself down on Blake's erection, as Blake pulled it away every time. When he was down teasing, Blake remained still, allowing Marc to lower himself slowly onto his throbbing cock.

Marc started tilting his pelvis forwards and backwards, rocking in rhythm to Blake's slow thrusts. Marc's hands rested on Blake's furry chest, running his fingers through the hair as they made love. Occasionally, Blake would pull Marc's face towards him and kiss him softly.

"Turn around," Blake softly commanded. Marc complied, pulling himself off Blake's dick and turning to face away from Blake. Blake pulled himself up so that he was reclined against the headboard. Marc lowered himself back onto Blake. Once he was fully involved, he leaned back against Blake's chest, turning his head to kiss his lover. They continued to grind against each other, enjoying the pleasure of intimacy combined with the perfect sexual partner. As Blake got close to orgasm, he wrapped his arms forcefully around Marc and rotated him facedown, his hard dick never pulling out during the move. Blake reached his right arm under Marc's neck, pulling back slightly to force a lordotic curve in Marc's back, pushing his firm ass up and into Blake's thrusts.

Blakes left hand found it's way under Marc and allowed March to fuck his hand as he fucked his ass. Their motions became quicker and quicker. Blake nibbled softly at Marc's ear as he came. "I love you." He whispered as his load emptied into his lover. Marc pushed back hard with his hips, forcing every last drop of Blake's juice inside him.

"I love you," Marc responded as his own load saturated the sheets.

Blake rested on top of Marc, allowing his penis to stay inside until it softened and exited on its own. He gently kissed Marc's back. After a few moments, Blake rolled off, and the two men faced each other. Blake's hand fingered Marc's tousled hair, caressing his face and kissing him gently. "You are my world, Marc. I'm so happy with you. So content. So at peace," Blake confided. "It's not just the mind-blowing sex. I just love being with you. You complete me."

"Ditto, my lover, my friend," Marc replied as he nestled his head on Blake's chest.

They quickly fell asleep, not bothering to clean themselves. Choosing instead to bask in the glow of lovers' contentment. A perfect end to another perfect day.

Saint-Clément d'Orque was not just a village; it was a sanctuary. It was where they had rediscovered the beauty of unhurried days, the joy of small rituals, and, most importantly, the profound connection that had carried them through decades of life's twists and turns.

Each evening, as the church bells rang softly in the distance, signaling the close of another day, Blake and Marc exchanged a smile, knowing that tomorrow promised more of the same quiet magic.

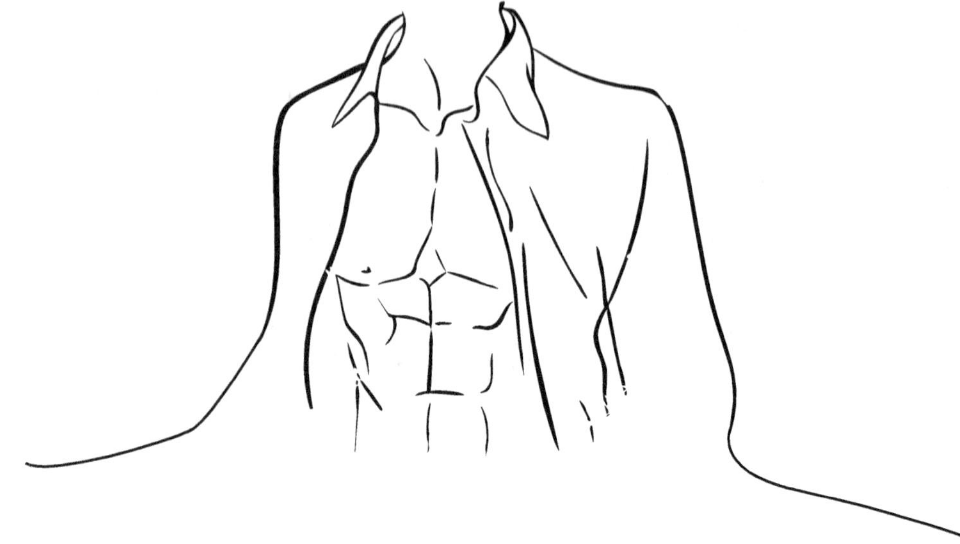

9: Unbuttoned and Exposed

Jaron greased the chain on his road bike with slow and deliberate focus. The room in the cheap motel was crowded with four guys and four bikes, and Jaron had claimed a small area between the nightstand and the wall to service his bike. The other three guys had similarly claimed areas in the small room. Mike had his bike centered perfectly between the two double beds, while Steve and Paul had each claimed space along the far wall near the small window that overlooked a dusty parking lot and the balcony walkways of another roadside motel. The four of them worked in silence, making sure their individual equipment was ready for the event that was a short two days away. Having traveled from Dallas, the four men had arrived two days early to make sure they were prepared for the strenuous ride ahead.

The Salt-to-Saint Relay was an event that Jaron had been anticipating for months. 421 miles in 24 hours. Beginning in Salt Lake City and ending in Saint George, Utah, the ride was a team relay.

Jaron had been training for months with Mike, Steve, and Paul. Their weekend rides were full of camaraderie and laughter, building bonds that only existed between guys who trained together.

"Hey, Jaron, you got some lube?" Mike asked, repositioning himself so that he was leaning over the bed towards Jaron. Mike had taken his shirt off earlier, and it had proven to be a significant distraction for Jaron. Mike was short and lean, his well-defined chest framing a small patch of dark hair in the center with a fine trail running down his navel and teasing at what might be in his shorts. His fit body, ice-blue eyes, and dark crew cut made for a very attractive combination.

"What?" Jaron asked hesitantly, running a hand over his shaved head and then along his full dark beard.

"Lube. For my bike chain. I can't seem to find mine," Mike shot back. "What kind of lube did you think I was talking about?" He winked and laughed as he took the small bottle of chain lubricant that Jaron was offering across the bed.

"Sorry, my mind was somewhere else," Jaron answered.

"No worries, my friend. I'm just messing with you," Steve joked as he returned his focus to his bike chain.

Jaron did the same, unable to resist glances in Mike's direction as he worked around his equipment. Mike's firm ass looked fantastic in the tight running shorts he was wearing. The slight bulge in the front had also not gone unnoticed by Jaron. He was having difficulty returning his focus to the bike as he thought about what might be in those shorts and how it would feel pressed against him.

"Ugh! Son of a bitch!" Mike yelled in frustration, looking down at the broken chain that had partially fallen to the floor. Mike grabbed the chain and pulled it completely off the cassette and threw it on the floor in frustration.

"I think I have an extra chain in my truck. And I need to get some air. I'll be back after I cool down," Mike addressed the three other guys in the room. Paul and Steve looked up and nodded.

"Hey, Jaron, want to help me look?" Mike asked casually.

"Sure, buddy," Jaron answered as he neatly placed his tools on the floor and followed Mike, who was already out the door. They walked in silence to Mike's truck. Mike opened the back door to the spacious crew cab Ford F-150 and climbed in, his firm ass directly in Jaron's face as he rummaged around under the back seat. As Mike moved further into the truck, Jaron leaned in and started looking through the bags of bike parts that Mike casually kept stuffed under the seat. In frustration at not finding the chain, Mike sat down in the seat.

"Sit with me for a minute," Mike said as Jaron fully entered the back seat, closing the door behind him. "I just need to catch my breath and calm down."

Mike's gaze focused on Jaron's face, imparting a cue that Jaron found difficult to interpret. Jaron could not help allowing his own gaze to drift to Mike's crotch. Mike's erection was clear and evident in his silkie running shorts.

"Care to help me relieve some tension?" Mike asked firmly.

Without hesitation, Jaron silently nodded. Mike hooked his thumbs in the waistband of his shorts and shoved them down to his ankles, revealing a cock that was short and thick. The head was large and pulsing with the strength of his hard-on. Jaron grabbed Mike's throbbing member and cupped his hand lightly around it. He started to stroke gently, allowing the grip to remain loose, his fingers brushing the dorsal ridge of the glans with each movement. Mike moaned.

"Fuck that feels good," Mike whispered.

"I bet I know what would feel better," Jaron responded, moving his mouth to Mike's cock. He sucked firmly on the head, flicking the underside with his tongue as his mouth moved up and down. His fingers gently teased the underside of Mike's balls, feeling them draw tighter as Mike got closer to release.

Jaron suddenly pulled back and stopped all motion.

"What the fuck are you doing?" Mike exclaimed.

"Promise me we'll do this again, and I'll finish," Jaron demanded.

"I promise, I promise," Mike said quickly.

Jaron grabbed Mike's rock-hard cock in one hand and fully immersed it in his hot, wet mouth. His other hand massaged Mike's balls, and he worked the head of Mike's cock with his tongue, the hand on Mike's cock moving up and down at the base.

"I'm going to shoot!" Mike yelled in a breathless whisper. Mere second later, he unloaded into Jaron's mouth. Jaron could feel the hot jizz hit the back of his throat as Mike shoved his cock deep into Jaron's moist mouth. Jaron swallowed it all. He loved this part of getting guys off.

"My god, that was intense," Mike said.

"Yeah, you definitely needed that," Jaron responded. "Glad I could help.

"Give me a minute to recover, and I'll return the favor, Jaron."

"I'm good, buddy, but how about I fuck you real good later?" Jaron asked.

"Deal. You better keep that promise. If you fuck as well as you suck, then I'm in for a real treat."

"I've had no complaints," Jaron smiled.

Mike pulled up his shorts and relaxed back in the seat. "Where and when?"

"Let's meet back here, in the back seat, after Paul and Steve are asleep," Jaron offered.

"Good plan. I'll be ready," Mike said.

As Jaron moved to open the door, he noticed something in the seatback pocket. Reaching in, he pulled out a new bike chain.

"This what we were looking for?" He asked, laughing.

"Yep, and I'm in a good frame of mind to put it on!" Mike laughed.

They returned to the room with the chain and focused on their individual bikes. Paul and Steve had no idea what had just happened. Jaron and Mike continued to share occasional glances and smiles, each looking forward to their planned rendezvous later that evening.

The four guys finished their bike maintenance and decided to walk to the diner across the street for dinner. They chatted casually about the upcoming ride. Jaron sat across from Mike. Mike would occasionally brush his bare leg against Jaron's, allowing it to linger, teasing at what would be coming later.

After dinner, the guys settled in to read, watch TV, and finish up with preparing for the ride. They still had one full day remaining before the event. Paul and Steve were sharing a bed. Paul sat propped up on pillows, flicking through channels on the TV. Steve was reading in the chair in the corner. Mike and Jaron sat in their shared bed, each on their phones, scrolling through social media.

"I'm going to call it a night, boys," Paul announced as he turned off the TV.

"Same," Steve said as he closed his book and made his way to the bed.

"I'm going to take a walk," Jaron said. "Just need to get some of this nervous energy out."

"I'll join you," Mike said. "I need to get a few things out of the truck, as well."

Before Jaron and Mike were even out the door, Paul and Steve were softly snoring. Jaron followed Mike to his truck in silence. Mike opened the door to the truck and motioned for Jaron to enter as he followed and closed the door. Jaron noticed that Mike had placed a towel on the spacious back seat, and there was a bottle of lube (the real kind) in the cup holder. When did he do that, Jaron wondered to himself. Jaron also noticed that the tint on the windows was dark enough to prevent seeing inside the truck, and Mike had placed a sun shade in the windshield so that they had complete privacy. Shortly after Mike closed the door, the cabin lights faded, placing them in almost complete darkness.

Mike did not waste any time. He quickly pushed Jaron back in the seat and straddled him. Jaron could feel Mike's hard-on pressed against his own. Mike placed his right hand on the back of Jaron's neck and pulled in close, their lips meeting with an intense sexual hunger. Jaron's tongue probed Mike's mouth, reaching his arms around Mike's waist and pulling him closer to him. Mike's left hand fumbled, trying to find how to get into Jaron's shorts.

Jaron pushed Mike off, inserted the fingers of both hands into Mike's waistband, and roughly pulled his shorts down to his knees. Mike wiggled slightly to get his shorts off before kneeling on the floorboard and returning the favor with Jaron's tight running shorts that were straining to hold in his massive cock. At the sight of Jaron's nine inches of perfect symmetrical dick, Mike gasped.

"It's perfect. And huge! Bigger than I thought. And I want it all," Mike said firmly.

Mike lowered his mouth on to Jaron's rock-hard dick and made slow, wet circles with his tongue, gradually taking all nine inches into his warm throat and savoring what he knew would soon be in his ass. Mike's left hand firmly encircled the base of Jaron's cock while his right hand moved slowly up Jaron's furry, flat stomach 'til he reached the right nipple. His index finger and thumbs played lightly with Jaron's erect nipple, producing moans from Jaron.

"That feels sooooo good, Mike. If your hole feels half as good as your mouth, then I'm going to go to bed very happy tonight," Jaron remarked.

"My hole is hot and tight. And I'm going to sleep better tonight once you unload in it," Mike responded, continuing to slurp at Jaron's knob before moving his wet kisses up Jaron's belly, to each nipple in turn, and ending at the nape of Jaron's neck where he kissed softly as he again straddled Jaron and positioned himself so that Jaron's hard cock was rubbing hard against his taint.

Mike reached behind him and grabbed the bottle of lube, pumping a generous amount into his palm and making Jaron's long cock slick before inserting a finger into his own hole to get it ready. All the while, he continued to kiss at Jaron's neck. Mike raised himself slightly to point Jaron's erection directly at his quivering hole, teasing himself with it. Mike moved his mouth to Jaron's and kissed him deeply as Jaron's dick, all nine inches of it, slid quickly into Mike's waiting hole. Mike took in a sharp gasp as Jaron's large penis penetrated him. Jaron and Mike both started to rock together, each finding the rhythm that allowed the entirety of Jaron's dick to penetrate Mike's hungry hole.

Mike kept both hands on the back of Jaron's neck, pulling himself closer with each thrust. Jaron placed his right hand on the small of Mike's back, guiding his hips as they rocked. His left hand found Mike's short, thick, perfect cock, keeping a loose grip to allow Mike to fuck his hand as Jaron fucked Mike's hole.

"Fuck you're good at this," Jaron said. "I'm getting close, don't stop."

Mike rocked his hips faster. Jaron let out a loud moan as he thrust his pelvis up into Mike, emptying his load where Mike wanted it. Mike ground down on Jaron, forcing every drop into him. Jaron, out of breath, collapsed back on the seat. Mike leaned forward and kissed him softly on the lips.

"How was that?" Mike asked.

"Fantastic," Jaron said breathlessly as he placed his hands on Mike's chest and pushed him back, maintaining his penetration in Mike's ass. Jaron interlaced his fingers around Mike's thick cock and started slowly stroking it, allowing the ridges of his fingers to massage the head. Mike groaned and continued to move his hips in small thrusts. He could feel Jaron's jizz leaking out of him around the massive cock that still pressed against his sphincter. Jaron removed one hand and ran it up Mike's belly, finding a nipple and squeezing it hard. He continued to stoke Mike's throbbing cock while moving his hand up to Mike's mouth, inserting his fingers where Mike sucked greedily on them. This took Mike over the edge. When he shot his load, Jaron kept his hand firmly around the base of Mike's penis. Mike's jizz shot up and arched through the air, landing perfectly on Jaron's face, covering his lips and chin. Jaron slowly extended his tongue and tasted Mike's sweet nectar. Mike leaned forward and kissed Jaron, extending his tongue and pushing his own load further into Jaron's mouth. They kissed, their tongues dancing in their mouths until it was all gone.

Mike pulled himself off Jaron and sat beside him on the truck seat, his left hand resting lightly on Jaron's thigh. They sat in silence for a few moments as they both recovered from the physical exertion.

"That was literally one of the best fucks I've ever had," Mike said.

"Yep, I'll agree to that," Jaron replied. "Your hole is magic. And the way you move your hips! I'm surprised I held out as long as I did." They both laughed as they wiped up with the towel and got dressed.

"You think the other guys will suspect anything?" Jaron asked.

"Probably not. But they will if we keep doing this. And I hope we do," Mike answered.

They exited the truck and made their way back to the room. They crawled into the shared bed with their shorts on, only removing their t-shirts. Steve and Paul were fast asleep. Mike rested his head on Jaron's chest and quickly fell asleep there. Jaron turned his head to the other bed, where he could see Steve, his tousled blond hair falling nicely on the pillow. Jaron drifted off the sleep, wondering what it would be like if the four of them could have a go as a group.

The next morning, the four guys woke at different times and each quietly worked at getting their gear in order. Jaron had found himself nestled into Mike's chest when he woke. He quickly looked at the other bed to see that Paul and Steve were still fast asleep. He turned on his side, facing away from Mike to appear that they had slept that way all night. Mike woke shortly after and made a quick assessment of the situation in the room before rolling towards Jaron and reaching around to find the cock that had given him such pleasure the evening prior. As his hand gently cupped Jaron's low-hanging balls, Jaron turned his head towards Mike and whispered, "Don't be naughty! They'll wake up soon."

"I'll stop when they do," Mike whispered in Jaron's ear as Paul stirred in the other bed. Mike's hand quickly retreated, and he rolled back to his side of the bed, but not before giving Jaron a quick kiss on the shoulder.

Paul sat up, swinging his feet to the floor and yawning with a big stretch of his arms over his head before noticing that Mike and Jaron were already awake. Jaron noticed Paul's physique through his tight t-shirt. He wondered what was under there.

"Morning, guys," Paul greeted.

"Morning," Jaron and Mike said in unison.

"I'm going to take a shower unless anyone else wants to go first?" Paul asked.

"Nope. I'm good. Still waking up," Mike answered.

"Go ahead, buddy," Jaron said as Paul stood and strolled to the bathroom. Jaron noticed a slight bulge in his shorts. Morning woody, maybe?

Steve woke moments after and bounded out of bed, stretching as he stood and showing off his toned, hairless chest and muscular legs. His boxer briefs stretched tight against his firm, round ass. He pulled on some shorts and quickly donned a tank top.

"I'm going to get coffee and some carbs. Shall I get something for everyone?" Steve asked.

"Coffee would be great!" Jaron responded.

"Yes, please," Mike added as Steve grabbed his wallet and walked to the door.

As soon as the door closed, Mike's hand was back on Jaron's crotch.

"Stop! They could come back in any minute!" Jaron warned.

"I'm willing to take the chance," Mike said. "So, Jaron, here's what's going to happen. I'm going to suck your massive dick. You're going to love it. So much, in fact, that you're going to cum quickly. Then Paul will be done with his shower, and Steve will be back with coffee. And that's how we're going to start the day. Got it?"

"Okay. I'll try, buddy."

Mike resumed stroking Jaron's cock, which had become rock hard while Mike had been whispering in his ear. Mike moved under the sheets and grabbed Jaron's cock with his left hand while flicking the underside of the head with the tip of his tongue. He could feel Jaron's dick pulse as he licked the throbbing head. He placed his wet lips over the head and slid them down to just below the ridge. Then back up again. He repeated this over and over, moving a little lower each time until he was fully taking all nine inches with each motion. Mike increased the suction in his mouth, using his tongue to flick Jaron's engorged head each time it passed his lips. Mike moved his right hand down under Jaron's balls and started stroking the area just above his anus, using increased pressure as he felt Jaron's balls begin to tighten. Jaron's tightening grip on Mike's shoulder let him know that he was ready to cum. With a muffled grunt, Jaron unloaded into Mike's hot mouth. As Jaron's orgasm subsided, Mike gently sucked every drop of Jaron's jizz, savoring the sweet and slightly salty taste as it slid down his throat.

They heard the shower turn off and Mike quickly retreated back to his position on his side of the bed. Jaron turned on to his side to avoid his re-emerging erection, a side effect of what had just happened. He could easily flip Mike over and have another go at that hot ass. The door to the room opened almost simultaneously as the door to the bathroom opened.

"Ooooh, coffee!" Paul exclaimed, emerging from the small bathroom with his shirt and shorts back on. Disappointing, Jaron thought.

"And sausage biscuits!" Steve offered, holding out a paper bag and a cardboard coffee carry-tray with four large coffees, steam rising from the vent in the plastic lids. Paul grabbed a cup from the holder as he walked past Steve to go sit in the chair by the window. Steve placed the bag on the end of Jaron and Mike's bed and handed them each a cup of coffee before sitting his own cup on the dresser. He opened the bag and doled out the individually wrapped biscuits, tossing one each to Paul first, then Mike and Jaron.

"Thanks, buddy. I'm famished!" Jaron said.

"I wonder why?" Mike mumbled under his breath as he looked at Jaron and winked. A gesture that went unnoticed by Steve and Paul, who were engrossed in eating their breakfasts. Jaron's right hand had been under the sheets and he lightly touched Mike's leg at the comment before withdrawing it and unwrapping his biscuit.

"What shall we do today?" Paul asked, his mouth full of the last bite of sausage and biscuit.

"What about a short run before lunch, then focus on getting our gear packed. I'd like to do a course preview for the local area. I heard the first hill is brutal. We'll also need to go over the relay plan, but we can do that over dinner," Mike offered.

"We also should get to bed early. We'll need to be up early to get to the starting line," Jaron added.

"Sounds good," Steve agreed.

"Ditto," Paul added.

Later that afternoon, their bellies full from a carb-heavy lunch, the four guys started packing their gear.

"I need to go out and get a few last-minute items," Steve said. "Anyone need anything?"

"Actually, I do need a few things. Mind if I tag along?" Jaron asked.

"No problem. Hey Mike, where are the keys to your truck?"

"Right here," Mike said as he tossed the keys to Steve and turned to give Jaron a sly glance.

Steve caught the keys and headed towards the door, Jaron tagging along behind. They rode in silence on the five-minute drive to the store. When they had parked, Jaron reached for the door but stopped as Steve's hand landed on his thigh.

"Let's talk for a minute, Jaron," Steve said as Jaron removed his hand from the door handle.

"Sure, what's up?" Jaron asked.

"I got up to pee in the middle of the night and noticed that you and Mike were snuggled up pretty close to each other. Anything going on that I should know about before the ride tomorrow?"

"Ugh. Well, we're not a couple, if that's what you're asking," Jaron replied.

"So what was that?" Steve pressed.

"Listen, it was just a thing last night. In this very truck. We had….. a moment. It was good, but I'm not sure it's relationship stuff. Just casual. You know what I mean?" Jaron fumbled over his words.

"Yep. I know exactly what you mean," Steve replied. " So… are you open to other casual 'stuff'?" Steve asked as he made air quotes with his fingers.

"With you?" Jaron asked.

"Yes, with me!" Steve exclaimed. "Is that such a bad thing?"

"Oh, no, my friend. I've frequently fantasized about doing 'stuff' with you," Jaron returned, using similar air quotes. Jaron looked at Steve's crotch and noticed that he was definitely up for something. He reached over and placed his palm on Steve's crotch.

"Is this what you're talking about?" Jaron asked.

"It's a start," Steve smiled, his own hand reaching over to massage the front of Jaron's shorts. Steve reached inside Jaron's shorts and slowly massaged his growing erection. To assist, Jaron pulled down the front of his own shorts and hooked them below his testicles, creating pressure that only accentuated his now full hard-on.

"Whoa," Steve exclaimed. "You're huge!"

Jaron did not respond. He put his head back against the headrest and moaned at Steve's expert manipulation.

"Show me," Jaron looked over towards Steve. Steve removed his hand from Jaron's cock and positioned his shorts in a similar fashion to expose his hard dick. Steve's cock was about the same length as Jaron's but much thinner, tapering to a smaller head. He was uncut, which surprised Jaron. Steve started stroking his own cock, retracting the foreskin to expose the fully engorged head. Jaron reached over and grabbed Steve's hand, placing it on his own dick, and he reached back over and started stroking Steve's.

Their heads turned towards each other, eyes meeting, staring. Jaron licked his lips as both of them increased the speed of their strokes. Their eyes remained focused on each other, moving occasionally from each other's faces to crotches and then back again.

"I'm close," Steve whispered.

"Me too," Jaron replied, as he focused on pulling Steve's foreskin over the head with each quickened stroke. Jaron's face contorted as he shot into Steve's hand. Steve followed seconds after. Their eyes maintained contact as they both came.

"That was nice, but I think I want more. Maybe after the ride?" Steve said.

"Yeah, I think that can happen," Jaron smiled. "Let's clean up and get the shopping done."

They used the towel that Mike had left in the truck to wipe up and exited the truck to go into the store. While walking around the store, Jaron could not help but fantasize about what it would feel like to feel Steve's long, thin cock up his ass. He imagined a long flip/flop session with Steve. He would have to make sure that happened after the race. Maybe Mike would be willing to join them?

Back in the room, the four men silently prepared for the ride. A quick dinner and into bed early, the focus was on the upcoming event and not on each other. Early the next morning, they loaded gear and bikes into the truck and made their way to the starting point. The next 24 hours showed that they could work as an effective and efficient team. The ride was exhilarating and exhausting. At the finish, they congratulated each other with hugs, slaps on the back, and a lot of jovial high-fives. They had arranged another hotel room for the next day and a half to recuperate before the 18-hour drive back to Dallas.

After finishing the ride, they stashed their gear in the locked truck while the four bikes were stacked neatly in a corner of the hotel room. Mike and Steve, eager to catch up with a mutual friend who had also completed the ride, headed out for dinner, leaving Paul and Jaron to fend for themselves.

Alone in the room, Jaron sat cross-legged on the bed, absently scrolling through social media. Across from him, Paul flipped through TV channels, searching for something to watch before dinner. Then, without warning, he shut the TV off and turned to face Jaron, his expression unreadable.

"We've been talking," Paul said.

"About what?" Jaron asked, getting a sinking feeling in his stomach.

"The other two guys said they've had sex with you," Paul explained.

Jaron blushed, not sure what to say. "Umm. They told you that?" Jaron replied sheepishly. "Why would they tell you that?"

"They were kind of bragging about how good it was. So what I want to know is," Paul said directly, "are you going for the complete set?"

"I wasn't planning on going after you," Jaron confided. "You didn't seem like you'd be very interested."

"Yeah, sex with guys really isn't my thing," Paul replied. "I've always been curious but never interested enough to try it."

"Understood," said Jaron, heading toward the bathroom with his toothbrush.

"But the other guys said sleeping with you was mind-blowing. Definitely in the top ten of sexual encounters."

"Oh yeah," Jaron said, a proud grin forming instantly on his face.

"So, maybe I'm a little interested," Paul countered, following Jaron to the bathroom. "I've always thought you were a good-looking guy.

Great build. Great smile. Friendly at work. I've always thought of you as someone I can rely on and trust. A great friend. Maybe we could solidify the friendship," he said, slipping his shirt off. "What would you do with me now that I'm shirtless," Paul asked coaxingly. Paul had a muscular build, with reddish brown fur lightly dusting his chest and arms. Jaron found this extremely attractive.

"Can I just show you instead of telling you?" asked Jaron, his heart skipping a beat. Of the three, he was most excited to see Paul with his shirt off. Paul's chest hair only accentuated his masculinity.

Jaron swallowed hard, his pulse thrumming in his ears as he set his toothbrush down on the sink. Paul stood in front of him, shirtless, the faint light of the bathroom casting soft shadows over his toned chest. His expression was unreadable—somewhere between playful and uncertain—but his eyes never wavered from Jaron's.

"Yeah?" Jaron asked, his voice lower now, edged with excitement. He reached out, his fingers grazing along Paul's stomach, testing the waters. "You sure you want to—"

Paul didn't let him finish. He stepped forward, closing the space between them, his breath warm against Jaron's cheek. "I think I do," he admitted, voice hushed. "But maybe you should convince me."

Jaron's heart skipped. Paul smelled clean, like soap and something distinctly him, and the way he was looking at Jaron—half-daring, half-intrigued—made the moment electric.

Jaron let his fingers trail up Paul's chest, feeling his heartbeat quicken beneath his palm. "No pressure," he murmured, but his other hand found Paul's hip, fingers curling lightly against the skin. "But if you want to know what the hype is about… you might want to close your eyes."

Paul let out a breathy chuckle. "That good, huh?"

"Find out for yourself," Jaron teased before leaning in, brushing his lips against Paul's in a slow, deliberate kiss.

Paul stiffened for half a second—hesitation, uncertainty—but then his lips parted, and he kissed back. Tentative at first, then firmer, as if his curiosity was winning out over his nerves. Jaron deepened it just slightly, his hand slipping around the back of Paul's neck, fingers threading through his hair.

Paul exhaled through his nose, pressing closer, his body warm against Jaron's. His hands found their way to Jaron's waist, gripping lightly as if grounding himself in the moment. The uncertainty that had been in his stance before was gone now, replaced by something hungry and unspoken.

Jaron smirked against his lips, pulling back just enough to whisper, "Still not your thing?"

Paul licked his lips, looking slightly dazed but amused. "I'm… not sure yet." Then, before Jaron could make another cocky remark, Paul caught his jaw and kissed him again—deeper, bolder this time.

Jaron groaned softly, backing them both against the sink as Paul's hands roamed his back, fingers dipping beneath the fabric of his shirt. Jaron took the hint, breaking the kiss just long enough to tug his own shirt over his head and toss it aside.

Paul's eyes dropped down, taking in his hairy torso. "Yeah… okay," he murmured as if confirming something to himself. His hands found Jaron's hips again, and then, with a flicker of a grin, he added, "I see the appeal."

Jaron laughed. "Oh, we're just getting started."

Paul's hands tightened slightly on his hips. "Then shut up and keep convincing me."

Jaron was happy to oblige.

Jaron smiled, running his hands up Paul's arms, feeling the subtle tension in his muscles. Paul was still figuring this out—still adjusting to the reality of what he was doing—but the way he was responding? That was genuine. And Jaron had no intention of rushing him.

Instead, he leaned in, pressing soft, open-mouthed kisses along Paul's jawline, down his neck, lingering just long enough to make him shiver. "You're way too tense," Jaron murmured against his skin. "Relax a little. Enjoy it."

Paul exhaled, his grip on Jaron's hips loosening just slightly. "Easier said than done," he admitted, his voice lower now, rougher. "This is... new."

Jaron pulled back just enough to meet his gaze. "Then let me make it easy for you." He took Paul's hands in his own, guiding them to his chest, then lower to his stomach, letting him explore at his own pace.

Paul hesitated only for a second before his fingers brushed over Jaron's skin, trailing down slowly. His touch was tentative, but there was no mistaking the curiosity behind it. "You're... warm," Paul muttered, almost to himself.

Jaron chuckled, stepping in closer, pressing their bodies flush. "So are you."

Paul let out a small, surprised breath at the contact, but he didn't pull away. If anything, his grip on Jaron tightened, his fingers digging in just slightly as their bare skin pressed together.

Jaron took the opportunity to kiss him again, slower this time, giving Paul the chance to sink into it. It worked. Paul's tension melted away bit by bit as he kissed back, matching Jaron's rhythm, his hands beginning to move more confidently over Jaron's body.

Jaron grinned against his lips. "See? You're getting the hang of it."

Paul huffed out a laugh. "Shut up."

Jaron nipped at his bottom lip. "Make me."

Paul's hands slid lower, tracing the curve of Jaron's back, his touch no longer uncertain. "I think I can do that."

Jaron groaned as Paul suddenly flipped their positions, pinning him against the bathroom counter, his hands braced against the sink on either side of Jaron's hips. "Okay," Jaron admitted, breathless, "maybe you don't need that much convincing after all." Jaron could feel Paul's erection pushing against him, as his own pushed into Paul.

Paul leaned in, brushing his lips just over Jaron's ear. "You're still talking."

Jaron smirked. "Then shut me up."

Jaron leaned back against the counter, his breath uneven as Paul's hands slid across his skin. There was no hesitation anymore, no second-guessing—just the two of them, heat simmering between them, and Paul's curiosity blooming into something more than just a fleeting thought.

Jaron traced his fingers along Paul's arms, feeling the tension and excitement thrumming beneath his skin. "You're really committing to this, huh?" he teased, his voice husky. "So, how far do you want to take this?"

Paul smirked, his hands slipping down to the waistband of Jaron's pants. "I'm not half-assing anything."

Jaron let out a breathless laugh. "Good, because I like when people are thorough."

Paul met his gaze, and for the first time, there was something other than playful teasing in his expression. There was want, there was need. And it sent a shiver straight through Jaron.

Slowly, deliberately, Paul reached for the button of Jaron's pants, unfastening it with a flick of his fingers. His hands brushed against

Jaron's hips, his touch featherlight but electric. Jaron exhaled sharply, his stomach tensing at the sensation.

Paul hesitated for a beat, watching Jaron's face, gauging his reaction. Jaron answered by reaching for Paul's waistband, mirroring his movements, pushing his own curiosity just as much as Paul was pushing his.

"You okay?" Jaron murmured, his fingers pausing, offering an out.

Paul swallowed, his jaw tightening slightly before he gave a small nod. "Yeah. I want this."

That was all Jaron needed to hear.

He leaned in, capturing Paul's lips in another deep kiss as he slowly slid Paul's pants down, letting his hands explore the firm lines of his body. Paul followed suit, tugging Jaron's pants lower until fabric pooled around their ankles, leaving nothing but skin between them. Jaron was surprised at the perfect shape of Paul's penis. It was absolutely average in size and girth but had a pleasing symmetrical nature to it. And a slight curve upward, which had always added an extra level of attraction for Jaron. As a bonus, Paul's testicles hung low, swinging gently with every small movement.

Jaron groaned softly at the feeling—Paul's warmth, his solid frame pressing against him, the unspoken hunger in the way their hands roamed. Paul's touch was cautious at first, but as he grew more comfortable, his fingers traced bolder paths along Jaron's body, memorizing the shape of him.

Paul let out a quiet, almost surprised breath. "The guys said you were large, but I had no idea that it would be this big. It might be more than I can take this first time. You feel… different than I expected." Paul's fingers encircled Jaron's erect cock and softly stroked it, savoring the sensation of touching another man's intimate area.

Jaron grinned, pressing his forehead against Paul's. "Different better or different worse?"

Paul's other hand moved down from Jaron's shoulder, gripping Jaron's hips with newfound confidence. "Better."

Jaron chuckled, his own fingers drifting over the dip of Paul's back, exploring the heat of his skin. "Told you I'd convince you."

Paul laughed, but it was softer this time, breathy, edged with something deeper. "You're doing a damn good job."

Jaron smirked, lips brushing against Paul's ear. "Oh, I'm not done yet."

Jaron ran his hands up Paul's bare chest, feeling the soft, warm texture of his skin beneath his fingertips. His chest was firm but covered in a light dusting of hair, a contrast that Jaron couldn't help but appreciate. He let his fingers trace over it, reveling in the way Paul's muscles shifted beneath his touch.

"You're enjoying yourself," Paul murmured, his voice rougher now, laced with amusement and something deeper.

Jaron smirked, pressing his lips to the curve of Paul's shoulder. "Yeah. I really am."

Paul exhaled, shivering slightly as Jaron's lips trailed lower, the sensation of Jaron's beard intoxicating against his skin. He started slowly placing lingering kisses along the edge of Paul's collarbone before dragging his mouth down across his chest. The warmth of Paul's skin, the faint scratch of hair against his lips—it all made Jaron's pulse spike.

Paul sucked in a breath when Jaron's tongue flicked over his skin, tasting the heat of him. Jaron took his time, mapping out every inch, moving lower, feeling Paul's breathing grow uneven under his touch.

Paul let out a soft, involuntary sound when Jaron's mouth closed around a sensitive spot just above his ribs, his hands gripping at Jaron's shoulders as if anchoring himself. "You're really into this, huh?" Paul muttered, his words slightly breathless.

Jaron grinned against his skin, pressing a teasing kiss to the center of his chest. "I like making sure people enjoy themselves. It really turns me on."

Paul's fingers of his left hand curled against Jaron's back as his right continued to explore Jaron's cock and balls. "You're definitely succeeding."

Jaron continued downward, his hands mapping the lines of Paul's waist as he kissed along his stomach, tasting the warmth of him, feeling the way Paul's muscles tensed and relaxed under his touch. Paul's breathing grew heavier, his hands moving up to Jaron's head as Jaron slowly lowered to his knees. When Jaron nipped playfully at his hipbone, Paul let out a low, shaky exhale.

"Jaron…" Paul murmured, his voice thick with something caught between desire and anticipation.

Jaron glanced up, seeing the approval on Paul's face.

"Jaron, I think I'm beginning to see what the other guys were talking about. You're really good at this. Teasing me. Making me want you so bad…." he finished breathlessly.

"Let's move this to the bed," Jaron commanded, standing while grabbing Paul's hand and leading him out of the bathroom. Paul silently followed, his hard dick brushing against Jaron's ass as they walked.

Once they reached the bed, Jaron pulled back the covers, slid under them, and pulled Paul in after him. They faced each other, Jaron's one hand remained entwined with Paul's while his other gently played with the hair just below Paul's throat. Paul's other hand had re-discovered Jaron's erection, his hand maintaining a firm grip but not moving.

"I want us to enjoy this. Just explore. I'm going to guide you, just tell me if I go too far or if you are uncomfortable. Deal?" Jaron's voice was soft and compassionate.

"Deal," Paul replied softly in Jaron's ear.

Paul moved his mouth to Jaron's and started kissing him softly, gradually increasing to a frenzied passion, as if Paul could not get enough of this new sensation. Jaron responded in kind. Jaron pushed Paul onto his back and moved down to Paul's perfect cock. Jaron's tongue lightly flicked at the shaft and balls, teasing and tasting as he explored. Paul's moans and groans belied his pleasure. Jaron slowly inserted Paul's pulsing cock into his mouth, letting his lips slide slowly down the curved shaft, pausing at the bottom before pulling up and making circles around the head with his tongue.

"Stop, stop. You're going to make me come. I don't want to come yet," Paul exclaimed.

Jaron stopped and moved his face up to Paul's, allowing his massive dick to push between Paul's thighs as he settled his entire weight on top of him. He started kissing Paul gently.

"I'm going to move on to the next thing. If you come, don't worry, I'll make you come again," Jaron said, looking Paul directly in the eyes.

"You almost made me come by saying that!" Paul said with a chuckle.

Jaron pushed himself down so that he was kneeling between Paul's legs. He grabbed a bottle of lube from the nightstand and gently pushed Paul's legs and knees into a bent position, the tip of his large cock brushing lightly against the inside of Paul's thighs as he moved. He squirted a generous amount of lube into his palm and threw the bottle on the bed beside him within easy reach. He greased up his own cock, his face showing his pleasure as he stroked it. Jaron then moved his lubed-up fingers to Paul's hole. He rubbed his fingers flat against

Paul's tight sphincter, making sure it was sufficiently wet before teasing the tightness with a single finger.

"Here's how this is going to work," Jaron instructed. "I'm going to play with your hole for a bit to get it ready. You're going to enjoy this. Just allow yourself to embrace the sensation. When I have it ready to my satisfaction, I'm going to place the head of my cock against it. When I say squeeze, I want you to squeeze the head of my dick with your anus. Squeeze until I say release. Then stop squeezing. When you release, I'm going to push it in a little and let it sit for a minute before repeating. This will make it much easier for you to take me since this is your first time. Understand?"

"Yes. I'm a little scared. And excited. Will it hurt?"

"Maybe a little, but the pleasure will be more than the hurt. If it gets too much, let me know, and I'll pull out and we can take a break before trying again."

Jaron placed the head of his now throbbing cock against Paul's quivering hole. He let it sit there for a moment, allowing Paul to enjoy the sensation of the slight pressure.

"Squeeze," Jaron said. Paul squeezed hard against the head of Jaron's cock as he applied gentle pressure. "Now, release." Paul released, and the entire head of Jaron's erect cock slid in with the pressure that Jaron was applying. There was a sharp intake of breath from Paul as a brief sensation of pain washed over him before being replaced by immense pleasure.

"It's so fucking intense!" Paul said.

Jaron moved one of his hands from where it rested on Paul's thigh to Paul's stomach. He rubbed upwards to Paul's chest, finding a nipple and tweaking it with his fingers. His other hand moved to Paul's testicles, gently teasing them with his fingertips. Paul groaned in pleasure.

"Okay, buddy, squeeze again," Jaron instructed. Jaron squeezed hard. "Now, release." Paul released and pushed his hips hard against Jaron, taking in Jaron's full nine inches in one motion. Paul gasped, and Jaron let out a loud cry of pleasure.

"Fuck! You really don't half-ass anything!" Jaron exclaimed.

"Yep, this is starting to feel really, really good. Now, fuck me. I want it. Make me come. And then make me come again," Paul said hungrily.

Jaron leaned forward and kissed Paul firmly on the lips, starting slow strokes of his cock in Paul's ass. They moved in perfect rhythm. Paul finding his pleasure while Jaron enjoyed the motions of a hungry, virgin bottom. Jaron repositioned to be upright, getting a small amount of lube before grabbing Paul's pulsing cock. He stroked Paul's member slowly, allowing his fingers to ripple across the head with each motion. It took mere seconds for Paul to come. He shot his load onto his own stomach, his head and back arched back with the intensity of his orgasm. When he had completely exhausted himself, he collapsed back on the bed. Jaron's cock, still hard and throbbing, remained inside Paul.

"That was the most amazing and intense orgasm I've ever had!" Paul said breathlessly.

Jaron did not respond. He just continued to rub Paul's sweaty body, savoring the view. He remained still for a few minutes before leaning forward and kissing Paul softly. He was surprised to feel that Paul's erection was returning.

"That was quick," Jaron said.

"It won't take me long to be ready again. Please keep doing what you were doing," Paul instructed.

Jaron, starting slowly, continued sliding his dick in and out of Paul's hole. Feeling the tightness massage his massive, hard dick. His motions quickened as he approached orgasm. With a final hard push, he unloaded in Paul's ass, his body shook at the intensity of having started, paused, and then finished. He collapsed on Paul, who wrapped his arms around Jaron, pulling him tightly into him. Their sweaty bodies sliding against each other as they kissed.

"When you've rested a bit, I want you to suck me off," Paul whispered in Jaron's ear.

"With pleasure," Jaron responded, moving to look Paul in the eyes, then resting his cheek on Paul's chest. A few minutes later, Jaron raised himself up and slid down to between Paul's thighs, taking Paul's re-erected penis into his mouth. Jaron worked Paul's cock methodically and slowly, savoring the taste of his previous orgasm and the new batch of pre-cum that leaked generously out of his dick. Using his tongue to work the head of Paul's cock, it did not take long for Paul to achieve his second orgasm. As he released his load of jizz into Jaron's mouth, Jaron savored the pulsing of Paul's ejaculation as he swallowed all of Paul's load.

With both of them satisfied - Paul twice, Jaron moved up to lie beside Paul, his head resting on Paul's chest.

"Next time, I want to try what you did. Are you okay with that?" Paul asked.

"I'd like that," Jaron responded. "And, hey, what makes you think there will be a next time?" Jaron laughed.

"Just making an assumption based on my own desires," Paul responded.

"Yep, there is absolutely going to be a next time," Jaron said.

Paul pushed Jaron back so that he could rest on Jaron's chest, where he quickly fell asleep. Jaron himself was drifting off when he heard the click of the door lock. Not wanting to wake Paul, he waited to see what would happen. Steve and Mike entered, paused, looked at each other, and smiled.

"So you DID complete the set!" Mike said emphatically. "How was it?"

"Amazing," Jaron responded. "Only one thing could make it better. You guys up for some fun later?"

"Yes!" Mike and Steve exclaimed in unison, awakening Paul, who sat up, startled and not knowing what to do.

"Relax, buddy," Jaron said as he pulled him back down to him. "The three of us have a surprise for you later."

"Uh, okay," Paul said. "Should I be scared or excited?"

"Both," Mike, Steve, and Jaron said together, as they all laughed.

Jaron and Paul quickly fell asleep in each other's arms as Mike and Steve got ready for bed. As Jaron was drifting off, he heard the sound of Mike and Steve having sex in the next bed. As he fell asleep, his thoughts turned to what would happen the next day.

The next morning, the four men had breakfast together, as usual, with no mention of the previous evening. They had decided to have a leisurely day taking inventory of their gear and performing necessary preventative maintenance on their bikes that would save time once they completed the long and tiring drive back to Dallas the following day. As the afternoon came to a close, they sat around the hotel room, each engrossed in their own activity. Jaron scrolling social media on his phone, Mike and Steve reading, and Paul flipping through the channels on the television.

"So, what happened to all this fun I was supposed to expect today?" Paul asked, turning off the TV and looking around the room.

"I'm up for some fun," Steve said, closing his book.

"Same here," Mike added. "How about you, Jaron? All this is centered around you, it seems." Mike smiled and winked at Jaron as he spoke.

"I thought you guys would never ask!" Jaron said with enthusiasm. "But first, let's set some ground rules. I don't want anyone to feel pressured to do anything they don't want to do." He glanced at Paul. "Can we go around the room and say what we expect from this? And guys, please be honest and direct. It will help us all have the best time possible."

"I'll start," Mike said quickly. "I Just want to get fucked by each of you. That simple. Anything else is a bonus for me. Everyone okay with that?" Paul just stared at Mike and nodded. Steve and Jaron acknowledged agreement with a nod, as well.

"Well, mine is more complicated," Steve said. "I want to fuck Mike and Jaron, and I want to get fucked by Paul." Paul again nodded his agreement.

"That takes care of at least one of mine," Jaron said. "I've been fantasizing about having your dick up my ass since I jerked you off in the truck. Other than that, I'm happy to fuck Mike and more than happy to do what ever Paul wants. But I really want you to fuck me, too." He started directly at Paul with this last statement.

"Okay then. That leaves you, Paul." Mike said, looking at Paul directly.

"It all sounds good to me," Paul replied. "I'm new at this, but really enjoyed being fucked by Jaron, and told him I want to try topping next time. So, I'd like to fuck Mike as well. As for Steve, I think I'm limiting myself by my one experience with Jaron, so I'd like you to fuck me, as well." He looked at Steve, who nodded agreement. "This may be a stupid question, but how do we start this? I'm already super hard."

"Stand up, Paul," Jaron commanded as he himself stood. "Come over to me and start kissing me." Paul complied, pretending that Jaron was the only one in the room with him. Soon after, Mike joined them, followed by Steve, the two of them removing their clothes as they joined. The four of them stood in a tight circle, kissing each other in rotation, with all four sets of lips and tongues meeting in the middle at times.

"Ah, I see how it works now," Paul said before taking Mike's tongue fully in his mouth.

Mike worked at Paul's clothes, while Steve worked at Jaron's. Soon, all clothes were off, and the four guys stood naked, four hard cocks rubbing against each other in the center of the circle. As Paul focused on kissing Mike, he reached down and grabbed Mike's short, thick cock. Paul was surprised at the electricity that coursed through him at being able to freely touch another man's penis. Now, he had access to three. The sensation almost made him come. Mike turned towards Paul and started slowly stroking his cock. Paul abruptly pushed Mike's hand away.

"I'm going to come if you keep touching it," Paul said.

"It's all good, Paul. The real question is—how many times can you handle coming tonight?" Mike responded. "Now, why don't you fuck me and shoot the first load up my ass. Really go at it hard and fast to get this first one out."

Mike positioned himself on the bed, face down, his hairy ass raised in the air. Paul grabbed a bottle of lube from the dresser nearby and squirted a small amount in his hand. Mimicking his previous encounter with Jaron, he made sure that Mike's hole was lubed up before applying it to his own cock. As he pressed his hard dick against Mike's hot, waiting hole, He expected a slow entry like Jaron had done with him. Instead, as soon as Mike sensed the tip of Paul's penis, he pushed back hard so that Paul's 5-inch erection was fully inserted.

"Now fuck me. Hard," Mike commanded. Paul complied, going at Mike's hole with reckless abandon. He pushed Mike down fully flat on the bed, reaching under him to touch Mike's hard dick. This took Paul over the edge. With one final hard push, he emptied his first load of the night into Mike's hungry ass. As Paul came, Mike ground his ass into him, making sure that every last drop was inside him. His goal of being the evening's cum dump was off to a good start.

As Paul lost himself in the moment with Mike, Jaron and Steve remained locked in their own embrace, their hands exploring, their kisses deep and unhurried. They stole glances at the scene unfolding before them—Paul fully immersed in his newfound pleasure.

Then, with a breathless chuckle, Paul seemed to find a second wind. He withdrew from Mike, rolling onto his back, his chest rising and falling with exhilaration.

"Next," Mike said, looking back over his shoulder at the other two guys. Jaron did not hesitate, lubing up his own cock and positioned himself to hover above Mike's ass, allowing his big, hard dick to tease Mike's hole.

"So that's how it's going to be, huh?" Mike joked as he pushed hard up against Jaron, forcing Jaron's cock inside him. Jaron's head arched back in pleasure at the sensation of Mike's tight, warm, hairy hole wrapping around his cock. Jaron grabbed Mike's shoulders and started slow, rhythmic strokes, enjoying the familiar feel of Mike's sphincter working him towards climax. Jaron reached under Mike's neck and pulled his face to the side so he could kiss him. Paul beat him to it, rolling to his side and inserting his tongue into Mike's mouth. Jaron's tongue soon joined them. Jaron's hand extended over and started gently caressing Paul's dick, which was again harder than he thought possible.

Steve, not wanting to be left out, lubed up his own cock and flipped Paul on his stomach. He extended his body fully on top of Paul. Paul could feel Steve's long, thin cock slide between his thighs. Steve raised himself slightly so that his hard cock was parallel to the two of them, sliding upwards along Paul's butt cheeks, teasing his previously virgin hole. Without warning, Steve's cock entered Paul. Paul took in a sharp breath at the sensation.

"Just breathe," Steve whispered in Paul's ear. Paul took deep breaths as Steve slowly fucked him.

Paul turned his head to face towards Mike, who moved his face forward so they could kiss. In turn, Steve and Jaron kissed passionately as they fucked Mike and Paul.

"What say we switch?" Jaron looked at Steve.

"Deal," Steve replied as he pulled out of Paul. "Your ass is hot, I'll be back at it later. You're going to get one of my loads before the night's over," he whispered in Paul's ear. Jaron moved on top of Paul as Steve started fucking Mike. Mike and Steve had a comfortable rhythm, clearly having enjoyed each other before now.

"You ready for this?" Jaron asked Paul as he positioned the tip of his cock at the entrance to Paul's hole.

"Yes, Jaron, Steve got me ready, just stick it in. No teasing like last time," Paul responded eagerly. Before Paul could even finish his request, Jaron smoothly and quickly pushed into Paul. Paul pushed back, enjoying the sensation of Jaron's big dick inside him.

"Just a few pumps, and we're going to switch. How do you want me?" Jaron asked Paul.

"Give more than a few, then I want you on your back so I can see your face as I fuck you," Paul responded with confidence. Jaron gave Paul more than a few pumps before pulling out and rolling over beside him, lifting his legs in the air so that Paul could see his waiting hole.

Paul grabbed the lube and positioned himself between Jaron's legs, arranging the tip of his throbbing cock on Jaron's hole. With little delay, he pushed it in, savoring the sensation that he had been wanting since their previous encounter. Paul took slow and deliberate strokes inside Jaron, not wanting to come too soon.

Steve pulled out of Mike and moved to behind Paul.

"Let's have some real fun," he said to Paul as he grabbed his shoulders and entered Paul from behind. As he pushed into Paul, Paul's dick pushed further into Jaron. Mike, not wanting to be left out, squatted on top of Jaron, facing Paul, as he lowered himself onto Jaron's big, thick dick.

"Grab my dick," Mike directed Paul as he leaned forward to kiss him, all the while rocking his hips on Jaron's cock. Paul did as instructed, his hand firmly around Mike's thick cock while Mike fucked Paul's hand with each movement of his hips. The combination of fucking Jaron, being fucked by Steve, and kissing Mike while stroking that thick cock took Paul quickly to the edge. Not being able to hold it any longer, he came inside Jaron, leaning heavily towards Mike with the intensity of the orgasm. His loud groans showed his pleasure. Simultaneously, Steve unloaded in Paul's ass.

"See, I told you I would finish in you," Steve said in Paul's ear as he pulled him away from Mike. Mike's hips rocked faster as he came closer to orgasm. As Jaron shot in Mike's ass, Mike came, covering Paul's hand with Jizz. Steve pulled out and pulled Paul with him down onto the bed. Mike collapsed back on Jaron. The four of them, exhausted, became a tangled, sticky, satisfied mess as they gently caressed and kissed each other in the aftermath of this intense session.

"That was unbelievable!" Paul said.

"Yeah, that was pretty fucking amazing," Mike added

"Yep, much better than I thought it would be," Steve chimed in.

"Ditto," Jaron said.

"You think we can do this again?" Paul asked. "I don't think I got everything I needed." They all laughed at Paul's enthusiasm.

"Yes, Paul, I think we're all up for more. Let's clean up and get some dinner. Then we will see where the evening takes us," Jaron responded to the group.

They took turns showering, all in the bathroom together, rotating through the hot water in changing pairs as they continued to fondle and joke with each other. The conversation frequently teased Paul on his new hobby. Paul took it in stride, not disagreeing with them. They finished washing, dressed, and walked across the street to a local pizza joint, where they enjoyed pizza and beer before returning to the room.

The after-dinner session was different from the first. There was more conversation, including many questions from Paul. There was also more intimacy, the group of four making the session last until the early morning as they enjoyed each other's bodies.

The drive home the next day was long, with each of them taking turns driving. They talked about many things on the drive. The conversation did not focus on the previous night's activities, but they did all agree that they wanted to do this again. All admitting that it did not need to wait for another event.

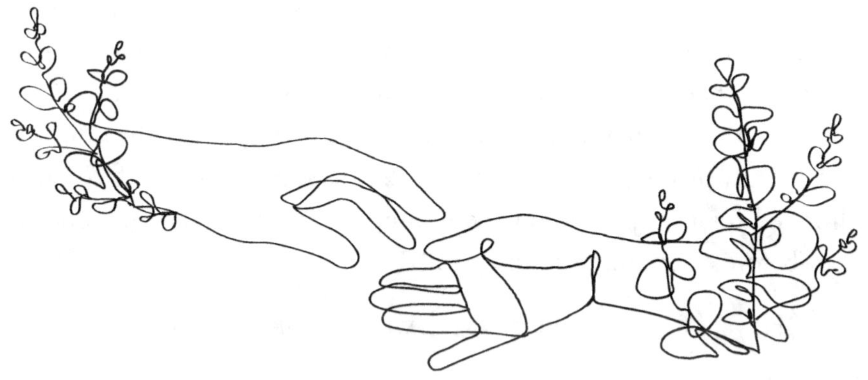

10: Encounter in the Bosque

The afternoon sunlight filtered softly through the canopy of cottonwood trees. Jake enjoyed this time of day more than any other for his Sunday rucks in the Bosque. The multiple trails along the Rio Grande River offered several options for both terrain and view. Today, Jake had decided to venture down closer to the riverbank, winding his way through the maze of ancient trees, various tall grasses, and false boneset. The 40-pound pack on his back felt light in the cool breeze and soft light.

As the trail meandered closer to the riverbank, Jake noticed a man standing near the water. The first thing Jake noticed about the man was the way he was dressed. Or, more specifically, how he was partially undressed. The man was facing the river, shirtless, wearing blue jeans, cowboy boots, and a ball cap. The fishing rod in his hand and a tackle box at his feet gave Jake the notion that this guy wanted solitude.

Nevertheless, Jake could not help notice the man's fit torso and how the well-worn jeans hugged his firm, tight butt cheeks.

As Jake approached, the guy turned and smiled at Jake. His well-defined chest was covered in reddish-brown fur at the top, tapering to a light trail that descended into a large metal western belt buckle sitting nicely at the waistband of his jeans. The guy touched the brim of his cap briefly, pushing it up slightly so that Jake could see his face, then dropped his fishing pole on the ground, securing it with one booted foot before extending his right hand.

"Hi ya, I'm Rory." The guy said, with an unmistakable Irish accent.

"Uh, you're not from New Mexico," Jake said, immediately embarrassed at his awkwardness.

"Nope. Ireland. But I've lived here for a few years now." Rory responded, smiling and clearly amused at Jake's awkward stammering. "What's your name?"

"Jake. I'm Jake." Jake responded, laughing at himself. "I'm not usually this incompetent."

"Nice to meet you, Jake," Rory said, grabbing Jake's hand and tugging hard, pulling Jake to within an inch of him.

Rory's dark green eyes stared directly into Jake's blues ones. Jake could feel the heat between them. He closed his eyes slightly, not sure if this guy was going to kiss him or bend him over and have his way with him. Suddenly, Rory released the handshake and stepped back, looking Jake up and down. Jake realized at that moment that he probably looked a mess. He was dressed in light-weight hiking pants with a long sleeve shirt, brimmed runners cap, and rucking boots. He had removed his sunglasses before Rory shook his hand but realized his beard and dusty clothes might make him look a little rough.

"So, rucking?" Rory asked, raising one ginger eyebrow to compliment his bright smile.

"Yeh, planning on 20 miles today. Just finished mile number two." Jake answered.

"Wow!. That's some distance!" Rory exclaimed, his irish accent, combined with that smile, caused a noticeable bulge to appear in Jake's pants. Jake noticed Rory looking. Was the front of Rory's jeans tighter than before? Jake couldn't help looking down at Rory's crotch.

"I'm training for an event, but sometimes I go running through here, as well," Jake responded, still feeling like he was fumbling over his words.

"I'll let you get to it, then," Rory said. "I'm here a few days a week. I like to fish and have some quiet time. Maybe I'll see you again." Rory winked, grabbed his fishing pole from the ground, and turned to face the river. Unsure what to do next, Jake resumed his walk.

The next day was a rest day for Jake. He had trouble focusing on his work at the design-build firm where he worked as a commercial architect. His mind wandered to thoughts of what that handshake might have turned into. Even just a kiss would have been nice. Jake pondered the potential size of Rory's most-likely uncut cock. He had never been with a ginger. What would that be like?

In the early afternoon, Jake called it a day and headed home, his attention being entirely consumed with Rory. The short drive to his house gave him enough solitude to imagine what he could do with this guy. Reaching down to his crotch as he drove, his right hand gently massaged the area of his tight slacks where his erection threatened to burst through the pliable fabric. Jake's dick was not huge but was slightly above average, or so he had been told. Several of the guys he had been with had commented on how perfect it was - not too big, not too small. Just the right girth with a well-proportioned head. Right now, however, it felt like the biggest dick in the world. When had he last been this hard? He couldn't remember.

Jake pulled his Mini Cooper Countryman into his garage and unbuttoned his pants before the garage door was even fully closed. He sighed with pleasure as he started slowly stroking his rock-hard cock. Thoughts of Rory sucking his dick and a few quick pumps was all it took to release the tension that had been building since the encounter the previous day. He shot his load with such force that it splattered the window. Jake threw his head back after his orgasm and turned his head to the left, and watched as his jizz dripped slowly down the glass. He would need to clean that up before it dried.

Sleep came easily that night. Jake drifted off, thinking that he would go for a run the next day and take his chances that Rory would be there. He woke early, jerked off before getting out of bed - this time with thoughts of fucking Rory's tight hairy ass, showered, dressed, and grabbed a protein shake from the fridge before making his way to the garage to get in his car and go to work. A soon as he sat down, he realized that he had forgotten to clean the window. Looking at the dried cum took his mind to what had caused it in the first place. Did he have time for one more? No. He would hold out.

Work was productive. He was on point with his team and, by 3pm, had managed to accomplish an astonishing amount. He knew the run that day would be good and he was ready to get to it and take a chance of seeing Rory again. He drove faster than usual on the way home and wasted no time changing into his running shorts, tank top, running cap, socks, and shoes. He stowed his phone in the back zipper pocket of his shorts and left his house. He walked the half mile to the trailhead and did some minor stretching before he started out at an easy jogging pace, being sure to take the same route down by the river as before.

And there he was. Rory was sitting against a large cottonwood tree, facing the river. As Jake slowed his jog, he noticed that Rory was also wearing running shorts and a tank top. Rory turned his head to acknowledge Jake, smiling as he stood.

"I wasn't sure if you would show up." Rory started the conversation.

"Yesterday was a rest day, and I drove home from work super fast because I was afraid I would miss you. But I really wanted to get a run in, and take the chance that you might be here. We didn't even exchange contact info." Jake blathered on, unable to contain his excitement at seeing Rory again.

"Slow down, brother," Rory said softly in his charming accent. "It's all good now that you're here. I'm happy to see you too!"

"Okay, okay, I know I talk a lot when I'm nervous and excited," Jake responded. "So, how are you?"

"I'm good. Better, actually, now that you're here." Rory seemed genuinely interested.

Jake moved closer to Rory, unsure what to do. Just seeing Rory has produced an erection that was clearly visible in the thin shorts. Rory reach out his left hand and gently cupped Jake's crotch, massaging the bulge with his palm.

"I guess you really are happy to see me!" Rory said, staring directly into Jake's eyes. "As you can see, the feeling is mutual." Jake looked away from Rory's mesmerizing gaze and noticed the fabric of Rory's shorts straining to contain what appeared to be a massive hard cock. Jake extended his left hand and reciprocated Rory's attentiveness.

"Listen, Jake, I don't usually do this kind of thing in public. Especially with guys I don't know. What say we meet for dinner tomorrow and get to know one another?" Rory's hand continued to massage Jake's erection.

"Same with me. What do you have in mind?" Jake asked.

"Meet me at el Patio on Rio Grande at 6pm tomorrow. Do you know it?" Rory suggested.

"Yes, one of my favorite places," Jake answered. "I can actually walk there from my house."

"Perfect. See you then." Rory abruptly removed his hand from Jake's crotch, leaned in, and planted a light and lingering kiss on Jake's lips, then took off in a jog. He glanced back briefly with a smile as ran away.

The following morning, Jake observed himself in the mirror after his shower. His body was not bad. Lean and slightly muscular, his light brown skin and small patch of dark hair on his chest gave a genetic nod to his father's New Mexican heritage. Jake always kept the hair on his head trimmed very short. Not shaved, just very short, which complemented his full, dark beard. Jake stoked his beard, still wet from the shower, his hand moving down to his chest, where he lightly rubbed the small patch of hair. As his fingers brushed across one nipple, he wondered how it would feel to have Rory play with his chest hair and nipples. This thought caused an immediate erection.

"Easy, boy. You have to wait. Hopefully, you'll be getting some attention tonight." He reassured his hard cock as it rested on the bathroom countertop.

Dressed in his favorite royal blue stretchy golf pants and a light-weight dark blue polo shirt, Jake found his mood elated as he drove to the office. The clothes perfectly complemented his tan skin and dark beard. The work day went quickly, requiring every effort to keep his mind from wandering. Nevertheless, his mind did wander. He was excited to spend time with Rory. He found himself thinking about the conversations they might have and not just the hot sex that he was hoping would follow dinner.

Jake arrived early to el Patio, entering through a wooden door to a rustic garden area with tables scattered around the perimeter under lean-to-like structures that provided a relaxing outdoor environment as well as cover from the elements. There was indoor seating, as well, in the small house that had been converted to a restaurant, but Jake preferred the outside seating. It felt more relaxed, with a sense of privacy amidst the otherwise crowded groups of diners. Looking around and not seeing Rory, Jake selected one of the only two available tables, thankfully in the corner, which offered some additional privacy.

After letting the waitress know that he was waiting for someone, he ordered a beer and settled back to wait. He did not have to wait long. As soon as the beer was placed on the table, Jake noticed Rory enter through the door to the patio. He was wearing boots, jeans, a western button-up shirt, and a cowboy hat. The way the Irishman looked in this get-up was intoxicating to Jake. And the "why" of that was one of the first things he wanted to know about him.

Rory scanned the patio and smiled when he saw Jake. That smile, combined with the way Rory was dressed, made Jake's heart flutter and his penis grow. Jake carefully arranged his legs to hide the growing bulge. As Rory approached, Jake extended his hand without standing. Rory shook the extended hand while sitting in the chair closest to Jake rather than across from him.

"Sorry, I didn't stand. Just didn't want to show the people what seeing you does to me." Jake laughed nervously.

"I understand, my friend." I had to sit quickly for the same reason. Rory reached quickly and quietly over, grabbed Jake's hand, and maneuvered it to brush against the hard bulge in Rory's jeans. Jake let his hand linger for a moment, then quickly retracted it, aware that others might see him fondling the crotch of another man in public.

"So, I have to ask -" Jake started the conversation, "Why the boots, jeans, and hat? I mean, I absolutely love it, and it looks great on you, but you're from Ireland, and this is not how I've imagined Irish people dress. And now I'm rambling again. Sorry."

"No worries, mate. It's a fair question." Rory responded, a big grin on his face. "It is totally a style choice. I've always been fascinated by the American West, and when I moved here from Dublin, I thought it was a perfect way to reinvent myself."

"Ah, that makes sense," Jake said. "Which brings me to my next question. What job do you have where you can dress like that and speak with that very sexy accent?" Jake laughed at himself for being so bold with his questions. But he really was interested in getting to know this guy.

"Well, Jakey, I don't wear these clothes at work. You see, I'm a physician, and I work at an urgent care clinic. So you would usually find me in scrubs. Which answers your next question of how I would have time during the day to be by the river. I work odd hours." Rory explained with a calm and patient nature that made Jake even more attracted to him.

The waitress returned and they both ordered green chile chicken enchiladas, and Rory ordered a beer, having already taken a sip of Jake's. There was a comfortableness between them that neither had previously experienced on a first date.

"Now that you know about me, let's chat about you," Rory stated, his smile gone and replaced by a kind and gentle gaze that showed sincere interest. "First, how old are you? Then tell me anything else you want me to know."

'Okay." Jake answered. 'I'm 34, just turned 34 last week, actually. I was born here in Albuquerque and never left. Although I have traveled. I went to school here for architecture and I work for a commercial design firm. I really like my job and the team that I work with. I have a good circle of friends, just no one to snuggle up with on chilly nights." Jake smiled at this last part.

"And why is that?" Rory questioned. "With your looks and personality, you could have any bloke in town."

"So they tell me." Jake laughed. "Just never found the one that clicked. You? You could clearly have your pick."

"Same, Jakey. Same." Rory seemed distant and thoughtful as he answered.

Rory's beer arrived, followed quickly by the food. They ate quietly, talking about mundane things that people usually talked about to get to know one another. Favorite colors - green for Jake, brown for Rory - which Jake found hilarious. Favorite comfort foods - posole for Jake, beef stew for Rory. As they finished eating and were enjoying fresh, hot sopapillas with honey, the conversation turned to more serious questions.

"Can we get something out of the way?" Jake asked a bit timidly.

"Of course. What's on your mind?" Rory responded, his tone serious and caring.

"What are you in to?" Jake continued.

"You mean, like, concerning sex?" Rory asked, knowing exactly what Jake was talking about.

"Yeh, you know what I mean." Jake smiled at him. "I mean, I'm not 'vanilla' by any means, but I'm not into kink or fisting or bondage or piss play, a dn things like that. Just creative, normal stuff. I like intimacy. That's what really turns me on. I mean, when you kissed me briefly that second day, I almost came in my pants. And the way you grabbed my hand when you got here and put it on your crotch - that stuff really turns me on. And now I'm going on like an idiot again…"

"First, Jakey, I like hearing you talk. So don't change that. Second, my tastes are like yours. I'm also versatile, so I like topping and bottoming equally. I just like letting things take a natural course."

"That's so good to hear. I'm also vers. When I was younger, I thought that I had to like topping better, but then I realized that I really only need to like what I like and find someone who is okay with that. By the way, you never told me how old you are? I'm guessing close me?" Jake was relieved at the direction this was going.

"I'm 35. So, how do you feel about dating an older man?" Rory laughed.

"So this is a date now, is it?" Jake laughed with him.

"Yes, Jakey, it is definitely a date. Do you want to come back to my place and see where this 'date' goes?" Rory asked forwardly.

"I walked here so we could go back to mine, or I can walk back and get my car and meet you at yours." Jake rambled, trying to figure out the logistics of this simple request.

"Or, you could stop overthinking it and just let me take you back to mine." Rory reached over and put his hand on Jake's thigh, squeezing it lightly.

"Yep. That's the answer." Jake smiled at him. "I can see that you're going to be good for me."

They rode in silence on the ten-minute drive to Rory's apartment. Even after Rory had parked, Jake followed him up two flights of stairs and into his apartment. Rory's apartment was simply and nicely furnished, clean, and comfortable. As soon as Jake closed the door, Rory turned and pinned him to the door, moving in close and pressing his mouth firmly into Jake's. Rory's tongue explored Jake's wet mouth as Jake returned the sentiment, his hand sliding down Rory's back and cupping that nice, firm ass. They kissed passionately for a few minutes, hands exploring each other's bodies. Rory placed his hands around Jake and hugged him tightly, his face dropping to the nape of Jake's neck.

"I've been wanting to do that for days." He whispered in Jake's ear. "Let's sit on the couch." Rory turned away from Jake, grabbing Jake's hand in the process and leading him into the living area, kicking off his boots and letting them fall where they came off. Jake kicked off his shoes in response. "Would ya like something to drink? Beer? Wine?"

"I'd love a glass of wine." Jake said. "Red if you have it. I love to kiss with the taste of red wine. Weird, I know."

"Not weird at all, Jakey. I know that sensation, and I love it as well." Rory reassured him.

Rory led Jake to the couch, a stylish retro-style in lime green, and pushed him back, straddling him and kissing him deeply before pulling away again. He really loves doing this, Jake thought to himself.

"Don't go anywhere. I'll be right back." Rory said jovially as he walked the few steps to the small kitchen grabbed a bottle of wine, a wine key, and two glasses before returning to the couch. Instead of sitting beside Jake, Rory kneeled on the floor between the couch and the wooden mid-century modern coffee table. Draping his arm over Rory's leg with the crook resting softly on Jake's knee, he opened the wine and poured generous amounts in the two glasses. Before rising, he kissed Jake's knee softly, then took a glass in each hand, extending one to Jake. Jake took the glass and raised it to Rory's with the typical clink.

"Here's to exploring new possibilities." Jake said.

"Sláinte!" Rory responded, smiling at using the traditional Irish toast.

Both took a sip of wine, Rory leaning back toward the end of the couch, extending his feet towards Jake, playfully poking at him.

"I could look at you all day long." Rory said in a low voice.

Jake did not respond. He took a large gulp of wine, carefully placed the wine glass on a coaster on the coffee table, and moved himself to be on top of Rory, taking Rory's glass out of his hand in the process and placing it beside his own. Jake allowed his full weight to rest on Rory. Taking Rory's head in his hands, Jake kissed him gently at first, savoring the feel of his soft, full lips, the taste of the wine on his tongue, the general musk of his body. Jake could feel Rory's erection pressing against his own, both cocks begging to be released from their prisons. Rory pushed his lips to the side of Jake's face, lightly kissing his cheek, then his neck, then moving slowly to the area just below the earlobe.

"Let's move this to the bedroom. I want to make love to you. I want it to be slow and last all night." Rory whispered in Jake's ear.

In silence, Jake allowed Rory to take his hand and lead him to the bedroom. They stood at the end of the queen-sized bed, facing each other. Jake failed to notice the simple wooden headboard, the overstuffed side chair, and the neatly kept nightstands. He failed to notice the solid brown-colored duvet and the neatly placed accent pillows. He failed to notice the soft lighting coming from the two lamps on the nightstands. Jake didn't notice the bottle of lube that was carefully placed on the right nightstand. All Jake noticed was the man before him.

Jake reached up and released the top snap of Rory's western shirt. As he reached for the second snap, Rory brushed his hand away and repeated Jake's action with the top button of Jake's own shirt.

"Let's take turns. Slowly." Rory said, staring into Jake's eyes. Rory then allowed Jake to release another snap. They repeated this process until both of their shirts were completely unbuttoned and hanging open. Jake reached forward with both hands and ran his fingers through the soft, ginger-brown fur on Rory's chest. Rory moaned with pleasure at the sensation, reaching out with his right hand to softly caress Jake's belly and chest. Rory extended both hands out to Jake's upper chest and slid his fingers under Jake's shirt, sliding it off his shoulders and letting it fall to the floor behind him. Jake reached up to do the same with Rory's shirt, but Rory brushed his hands away and stepped back a few feet.

"Just watch." Rory commanded as Jake's gaze moved from Rory's eyes to his chest to his crotch and then back again.

Rory slowly shrugged his shoulders so that his shirt fell to the floor. He then reached a hand down to his belt buck and released it with a quick motion of his fingers. He slowly pulled the leather belt out of the belt loops and dropped it on top of his shirt. His right hand moved back to his crotch and gently massaged his hard dick thru his pants before undoing the button of his jeans and slowly lowering the zipper. Jake could now see the bulge pop forward, still restrained by Rory's white boxer briefs.

Jake seriously thought he was going to come in his pants at this tease.

"Your turn. But stop before you show it to me." Rory said.

Jake repeated Rory's actions, although a bit more quickly. He wasn't as adept at this as Rory and was eager to see what was in Rory's pants. But he complied with Rory's request and stopped after lowering his zipper, his erection extending beyond the waistband of his dark blue briefs. The throbbing head of Jake's dick was visible to Rory, who licked his lips in anticipation.

"Show it to me." Rory said.

Jake swiftly pushed his pants and underwear to his ankles, finally freeing his rock-hard cock, which bobbed slightly with the release and arousal.

"My god, it's perfect." Rory reacted, quickly pushing his pants and underwear down as well. Jake stared at Rory's cock with a building hunger. Average length and very thick, with the foreskin pulling half way back on the head from the force of his erection, Rory's cock was bright pink with a thick tuft of reddish brown hair covering his entire pubic area and balls.

Rory stepped forward, pressing himself into Jake, grabbing Jake's ass cheeks as he kissed him deeply. Their cocks pressed into each other as Rory proceeded to grind against Jake. Rory pulled back and dropped to his knees, quickly taking Jake's firm dick into his warm, wet mouth. Rory let Jake's cock sit in his mouth for a moment, savoring the taste and smell. As Jake placed his hands on Rory's shoulders, Rory started moving his tongue around Jake's penis, making circles along the shaft as he moved his lips up and down.

"Stop. You're bringing me very close." Jake said as he pushed Rory back. "Let me have a turn." He smiled as he dropped to his knees as Rory stood.

Jake took his time exploring Rory's beautiful, erect dick. First, Jake cupped Rory's balls, enjoying the feel and texture of the hair and skin. He wrapped his fingers around the base and slowly licked the head, running his tongue under the foreskin, slowly pushing it back, and continuing to massage the entire head with his tongue. Rory's moans and groans let Jake know he was enjoying this. Jake placed his lips lightly around the head, very slowly moving them down the shaft. Rory's cock was so thick Jake almost could not get it fully into his mouth. He had no idea how it was going to be going up his ass, but he would cross that bridge when he came to it.

Just as Jake had done with him, Rory pushed him back, not ready to end this first part of the evening by coming too quickly.

"Let's get into bed." Rory suggested as he moved to the side of the bed and pulled down the duvet and top sheet. Rory slid under the sheet and motioned for Jake to join him. Jake slid in next to Rory, facing him. As they moved closer, the tips of their cocks playfully touched while they continued to kiss and caress each other.

"How do you want to do this?" Rory asked. "I know I'm thick, and I'm afraid that will be a problem."

"It won't be. We may just have to take it slow, and you will need to be patient. But I think you would anyway." Jake reassured him. "Is it okay if I fuck you first? I've been thinking about that for days!."

"I was hoping you would say that." Rory said. "I've been craving the feel of your perfect cock up my ass since I saw it earlier."

Jake rolled on top of Rory, kissing him in the process. Once he was on top, Rory pulled his knees up as Jake's hips slid down between them. Jake raised up on his knees, running his hands along Rory's torso and down to his pelvis, where he let his hands rest as his hard cock teased Rory's hairy hole. Jake reached over to the nightstand and pumped a generous amount of lube into his palm. He allowed a small amount to drip onto Rory's pulsing cock before rubbing the rest between Rory's thighs, his fingers gently massaging the slickness into Rory's hole, getting it ready for penetration. What was left on Jake's hand, he rubbed onto his own throbbing dick. As he positioned the tip of his erection against Rory's quivering hole, Jake leaned forward as he entered Rory. When his cock was fully inserted, Jake allowed it to sit for a moment while he kissed Rory's belly and chest. Jake could feel Rory's hard dick flexing against his belly. Jake kissed Rory on the mouth, their tongues intertwining as Jake methodically slid his hard cock in and out of Rory's accepting hole. Jake maintained a tight grip around Rory's thick cock as he pumped Rory's ass. Rory's hips rocked in rhythm to Jake fucking him, and he fucked Jake's tight grip.

Rory's kisses became more passionate as he got closer to climax. "I'm going to shoot!" Rory exclaimed. Jake kept contact with his mouth and continued to fuck him as Rory shot his load into Jake's hand, the cum covering their touching bellies. The feel of Rory's warm jizz brought Jake to the edge as he came hard with one final thrust. His ample load emptied into Rory's hole. Rory pushed his hips onto Jake, taking in every drop.

Jake collapsed as Rory reached his arms around Jake and pulled him tight into him, kissing his neck and face. Jake rolled on to his back and grabbed Rory's hand, interlacing his fingers as they both recovered.

"That was feckin' amazing!" Rory said breathlessly, his accent stronger than usual, as he rolled over onto his side and placed his hand on Jake's chest.

"For sure." Jake agreed. "I love your body, Rory. I loved holding your thick cock. That alone made me come super quick."

They rested for a few minutes, and Jake was just drifting off into a nap when Rory sat up suddenly. "I want a snack!" He said with excitement. "I'll be right back."

A few second later, Rory stood at the end of the bed, naked, his thick, flaccid cock hanging nicely against his balls. In one hand, he had the two wine glasses and the bottle of wine, which was being held precariously by the neck between two fingers. In the other hand, there was a bag of something that Jake did not recognize.

"What are 'Tayto Crisps'?" Jake asked, squinting at the bag.

"Oh, my friend. You are in for a treat. My mom sends me these from Dublin. Cheese and onion. My favorite!" Rory grinned as he threw the bag to Jake. "Try one while I pour us some wine."

Rory poured the wine, placing a glass carefully on coasters on each nightstand.

Jake examined the bag of crisps, which looked like one of Jake's favorite childhood treats. And one that he had not had in years.

"These look like Munchos," Jake remarked.

"What are those?" Rory asked.

"I think maybe the American version of Tayto Crisps, but just a plain flavor. I don't remember Munchos coming in any flavor other than potato." Jake answered.

Jake and Rory both took a sip of wine as Rory settled back to leaning on Jake's chest. Jake opened the bag of crisps and Rory looked on with anticipation. Jake looked inquisitively in the bag, then back at the outside of the bag, then back in before taking a sniff.

"Okay, buddy, taste them or give them up!" Rory said impatiently with a laugh.

Jake reached in and, grabbed a crisp, and extended it towards Rory's mouth. As soon as Rory opened his mouth to take it, Jake quickly put it in his own mouth."

"These are delicious!" He said while still chewing and pulling another crisp out of the bag. This time, Rory grabbed Jake's wrist and took the crisp by force with his mouth. They both laughed hysterically.

"You are a tease, Jakey!" Rory said through the laughter.

"Me?!" Jake responded. "Do I need to remind you about the past week? You're the tease. And you deserved that for making me wait!"

"True. True." Rory agreed.

They drank wine, ate Tayto Crisps, chatted, and cuddled for the next hour, finding being with each other familiar and comfortable.

"Stay the night." Rory said.

"Okay. On one condition." Jake replied.

"Name it."

"Fuck me. Make love to me. Then I'll stay."

"With pleasure." Rory smiled, clearing the bed of the crisp bag and wine glasses as he reached under the cover to find Jake already rock hard.

"I can see you're ready!" Rory said softly as he rolled on top of Jake.

Rory grabbed Jake's wrists and positioned them on the pillow beside Jake's head, holding them firmly but not too tight. Rory kissed him, slightly pulling at Jake's lower lip, exploring more of Jake's mouth. Rory reached for a pump of lube and liberally greased up his thick cock. He moved both hands back to Jake's, interlacing their fingers as Rory's thick dick slid between Jake's closed thighs. Jake could feel the foreskin of Rory's cock teasing his taint with the frottage.

"I want to be on top." Jake said. "Is that okay?"

"Of course. I can't think of anything better than watching you stroke your cock while mine is up your ass." Rory admitted.

Rory rolled onto his back, and Jake nimbly straddled him, grinding down on Rory's big cock. He liked the feeling of it stroking along his crack and teasing his hole.

"I want you inside me. But we need to take it slow. You're so.... thick." Jake said. "I've never had anyone with your girth. Not that my list is that long. Just take it slow, okay?

"Okay, Jakey. You're in control. I won't push unless you ask me to. You make it happen at your pace. Now kiss me." Rory commanded. Jake complied, leaning forward, his hands on Rory's chest as he continued to grind against Rory's pulsing erection.

Jake positioned his hole so that the head of Rory's hard cock was applying gentle pressure. He could feel his sphincter tighten under the pressure. He took a deep breath, held it for a few seconds, and released it slowly. He could feel his anus loosen. Jake looked down at this beautiful, gentle man beneath him and felt his entire body relax. With slow and careful motion, Jake allowed Rory's cock to enter him. There was a moment of intense pain that quickly turned to pleasure as Rory's full six inches of thickness entered him entirely. Jake arched his back, extending one hand behind him as he allowed his tight hole to adjust to Rory's size. Jake extended his other hand behind him, arching his back more and thrusting his hips forward to work Rory's cock.

Rory reached out and traced his hands down Jake's stomach, ending at his rock-hard dick that was bobbing up and down with each hip thrust. Gaining a loose grip, Rory let Jake fuck his hand as he bucked like a bronco on top of him. Rory felt Jake's balls tighten as he neared orgasm. He released his grip on Jake's cock, sat up slightly, and pulled Jake forward until they were both sitting upright. Rory held Jake tightly with his left arm wrapped around Jake;s neck as he thrust his own hips up hard into Jake. His right hand regained its grip on Jake's cock, and they rocked in unison, Jake's face pulled tightly into the crook of Rory's neck.

"I'm close." Jake whispered.

"Me too." Rory said back as he thrust one last time and shot his load inside Jake. As he emptied his jizz into Jake's ass, Rory felt the warm wetness of Jake's climax as it saturated his hand. Jake's entire body trembled as his orgasm subsided. His teeth had taken a firm bite into Rory's shoulder as he came. Rory did not seem to have noticed, but Jake was sure it would leave a mark. The orgasm had been so intense!

They collapsed on the bed, too exhausted to move. After a few moments, Jake rolled over to face Rory.

"That was the most intense sex I've ever had." Jake admitted.

"Same." Rory mirrored. I wasn't expecting it to be that hot. Now, shall we shower?"

Rory straddled Jake, gave him a big, wet kiss, and got out of the bed, taking Jake's hand and pulling him to the shower. They showered together, washing each other and talking about mundane things, such as what they liked for breakfast - porridge with fruit for Rory and Oatmeal with butter and salt for Jake. It took them a minute to realize they were talking about the same thing, which caused raucous laughter in the shower. When they finished showering, they dried each other off with the plush towels that Rory had stacked on a small table between the toilet and the large walk-in shower.

After they were sufficiently dried off, they returned to the bed, snuggling under the covers, Jake's head resting on Rory's chest as Rory stroked his shaved head and Jake fingered the hair on Rory's chest. They talked until they fell asleep.

When they woke early the next morning, Rory was spooning Jake, his arm draped loosely over Jake's midsection.

"Rory?"Jake called out softly.

"Yes, Jake," Rory answered, pulling him closer.

"Are you working today?" Jake asked.

"Not during the day. I have a night shift starting at 11pm. It's the down side of my job. I work two of these every ten days. So I'll need to take a nap in the afternoon. Why do you ask?" Rory was matter-of-fact in his statement.

"Do you want to spend the morning together? I can call out sick to work." Jake asked hesitantly.

"I'd like that a lot." Rory replied.

Jake grabbed his phone from the nightstand and sent his boss a text letting him know that he had a personal matter to attend to and would not be in today. His team worked well together, and they were okay with each other taking occasional personal days.

"Done." Jake said with a smile.

"So what should we do?" Rory asked.

"Let's walk to the coffee shop and have breakfast. Then, come back here and get to know each other. How's that? Jake suggested.

"Sounds perfect." Rory responded. "I especially like the idea of getting to know you better." Rory started kissing Jake's earlobe, gently flicking it with the tip of his tongue.

"Okay, tiger. You'll get some of that when we get back. Right now, I need coffee." Jake said, turning towards Rory and giving him a kiss before getting out of bed. As Jake pulled on his underwear and from the day prior, Rory could not help but feel a sense of calm satisfaction at how content he was after just one night with this guy. Could he be the one?

The walk to the coffee shop was pleasant. Coffee and breakfast burritos turned the conversation to things they would definitely not be doing back at the house. When they arrived back at Rory's apartment, Jake suggested they go to his house since he needed a ride home anyway. So they got in Rory's truck and drove the five minutes to Jake's house. Considering how neat and orderly Rory's house had been, Jake was unsure how Rory would react to his lower level of order.

Jake's house was an older adobe home that he had remodeled two years ago. The basic-old New Mexico character remained but had been updated by adding a second bathroom, a new kitchen, and eclectic modern design elements that only an architect would choose. The result was a funky two-bed, two-bath home that reflected the personality of its owner. Like Rory, Jake kept the same things in the same place. Unlike Rory, those places didn't always make things look neat. Dirty dishes remained in the sink until there were enough of them to load the dishwasher. The bed remained in a constant, un-made state until the sheets were changed. And the side table by Jake's favorite chair in the living room contained a collection of things that occupied Jake's time in the evening - books, snacks, unopened mail, an empty box from a recently delivered package, and other items that just never seemed to be put in their proper place. A drafting table took up space in the corner of the living room, covered in papers and tools expected from a creative mind. While clean, the house had a distinct "lived-in" look to it.

"I'm not as good at putting things away as you are. Sorry for the mess." Jake apologized.

"No worries, Jakey. I'm not judging. People live on their own terms in their own space." Rory reassured him with a smile. "Nevertheless, I'm happy to see where you live."

"This must be where you spend your evening." Rory said, walking over to the big, leather easy chair that was placed at an angle to an old and very comfy-looking sofa.

"Yep. That's were I settle in for the evening." Jake responded. "I usually need to do several things at once, so I have the TV on while reading or, drawing, or surfing social media."

"Have a seat and show me." Rory said.

"What?" Jake didn't understand.

"Sit in the chair, Jakey, and read a book. Let me see." Rory clarified.

"Okay. Weird, but okay." Jake smiled, having a feeling he knew where this was going.

Jake sat in the chair and, grabbed a book from the side table, and pretended to read. Rory quietly removed his own shoes, pants, and underwear, standing behind the chair where Jake could not see him. He moved around to the front of the chair and kneeled between Jake's legs, slowly reaching out to the front of Jake's pants and gently rubbing the growing erection there. He unbuttoned Jake's pants and lowered the zipper, moving slowly. He continued to pull Jake's pants down, and Jake assisted by slightly shifting his hips to allow the pants to be removed. Jake closed the book and started to put it on the side table.

"No, No, Jakey. Keep reading." Rory scolded. Jake re-opened the book.

His now rock-hard cock fully exposed, Jake took a peek over the top of the book. Rory was examining Jake's penis as if it were a rare treasure. Rory softly stroked it with the back of his hand, letting the ridges of his knuckles drift over the ridge of the head and then the entire length of the underside, ending with his fingers lightly tickling the soft fuzz that covered Jake's balls. Jake threw his head back in pleasure at the sensation. Rory's hand encircled Jake's shaft with a light touch, moving up and down while barely touching the skin. He tightened his grip slightly at the top so that his fingers would stimulate the head. Jake had never been teased like this. The sensation was magical, sending waves of endorphins through his body.

Rory removed his hands from Jake's dick and placed them palm down on Jake's belly. As Rory moved his hands slowly up Jake's torso to his nipples, he lowered his mouth to Jake's waiting, hard cock. With a nipple engaged by each hand, Rory slid Jake's cock fully into his wet mouth, letting it sit with his lips at the base as he flexed his throat around the head. Sounds of ecstasy from Jake let Rory know he was doing something right.

Rory started moving his mouth up and down Jake's shaft, flicking the head with the tip of his tongue each time Jake's head threatened to escape Rory's hot mouth. Rory continued to rub Jake's erect nipples between the thumb and forefinger of each hand. Jake started moving his hips as his orgasm became imminent. Rory's mouth moved faster, now providing a small amount of suction with each movement. Jake could hold it no longer. He threw the book on the floor and grabbed Rory's shoulders as his climax wracked his body. Rory took all of Jake's load down his throat, licking and sucking every last drop of what remained as it leaked out. Jake collapsed back into the chair. Rory stood and straddled Jake, his own hard cock pressing against Jake's belly as they kissed.

"Let me take care of you now." Jake said.

"I want something a little different if you're up to it." Rory responded.

"Okay, babe. Anything you want." Jake agreed.

"I want to jerk off in this position. While you kiss me and my nipples, in turn. Also, if you can rub my testicles, it will make be come super fast." Rory instructed. "I know it's weird, but it's something I like. Okay?"

"I like that. Let's do it." Jake smiled and then kissed Rory hard while he reached one hand down and gently cupped Rory's balls.

Rory grabbed his own cock and started slowly stroking it, his grip loose, as he had done with Jake. Jake moved to Rory's right nipple, then to his left, then to his lips, repeating this rotation while his fingers gently rubbed the area underneath Rory's balls.

"My god, you do that perfectly," Rory exclaimed breathlessly.

Jake focused on the pattern, which brought Rory to the edge within seconds. Rory exploded on Jakes chest with a loud exclamation of pleasure, then collapsed on Jake, his head nestled into Jake's neck and his hand still gripping his cum-wet cock.

"That was perfect," Rory whispered.

"That was super hot," Jake admitted. "When you've recovered, let's shower. Then, you're going to need to get back home and rest before your shift.

"I know, Jakey. Can I tell you something?" Rory reacted.

"Of course, Rory. What's up?" Jake's voice was kind and inquisitive.

"I don't know what this is or what it's going to be, but you're different. This is different. It feels comfortable to me. And that scares me." Rory became suddenly emotional." What I'm feeling right now is that I don't want to leave you. I feel pain at thinking that I have to be away from you for even a day. Is that normal?"

"Rory, it's probably not normal. But I feel the same. So, let's just go with it and see where it goes. Deal?" Jake mirrored Rory's emotions, not telling Rory that he, himself, was also scared. "Let's take a couple of days and meet again and see if we feel the same way. What do you think of that?"

"I think that's a good idea. Now, Let's shower. I want to enjoy the few minutes I have left with you today." Rory answered.

They showered, touching, kissing, caressing each other. Jake would occasionally just hug Rory, pulling him closely, preparing himself for not seeing him for several days. When they were dressed, Rory grabbed his keys and headed to the door. He hugged Jake fiercely. kissing his lips, then his neck. The look of sadness on his face reminded Jake that the next few days would be difficult.

"Let's meet on Satruday. In the Bosque where we first met. 10am. Good?" Rory suggested.

"Yep." Jake said as Rory walked out the door. A single tear escaped Jake's eye as he watched Rory drive away, realizing that they had never exchanged contact info but clearly knew where each other lived. It was an odd sensation, the feeling of longing combined with expectation.

The next few days were brutal for both men. They struggled to focus on work, wondered what the other was doing, and not having any way to check in unless they drove to the other's house. Thoughts of stalker behavior aside, they made it through, and Saturday morning arrived with pleasant weather and blue skies.

Jake dressed in running pants, a t-shirt, and a ball cap for the walk to the Bosque. He tried to walk slowly, knowing that he would arrive earlier than 10am if his pace kept increasing. The excitement was building with each step. Occasional thoughts of Rory not showing up invaded his mind. Typical to his practical nature, he pushed the thoughts aside, choosing to deal with that scenario if it happened and not otherwise.

As Jake approached the spot where they first met, he saw Rory leaning against a tree and staring out at the river. Boots, jeans, t-shirt, cowboy hat. Rory looked up as he heard Jake approach, his smile widening to the grin that melted Jake's heart. Jake ran the remaining distance to Rory, wrapping his arms around him and kissing him passionately. He tucked his face into the nape of Rory's neck and sobbed softly.

"I wasn't sure what I would do if you didn't show up. We didn't exchange contact info and I didn't want to be a stalker and drive by your house. I missed you so much, it hurt so bad. I couldn't focus at work. I'm so happy to see you." Jake blathered.

Rory pushed Jake away slightly and grabbed his face with both hands. "I know, Jakey, I know. It was the same for me. I actually did drive by your house. I just needed to feel close to you."

"Rory, I don't care if this is moving fast. I don't want to feel that pain again. I want to jump in feet first and see where this goes. I'm sorry if that's too much for you." Jake was hoping this did not scare him away.

"Jake, Jake, Jake. Slow down. It's okay. I feel the same way." Rory's words and tone were reassuring. He kissed Jake softly and pulled him close. "Now, before we get into this predicament again, send me your contact info."

Jake laughed as he pulled out his phone. "Good idea. Let's go have some lunch and talk about where we go from here. el Patio?"

"Perfect. You're perfect. Perfect for me," Rory replied.

"Same, Rory. So much the same."

Acknowledgements:

Special thanks to my husband, Shayne, for inspiration and for his never-ending support (and hot sex).